Portrait of the Artist as a Young Corpse

... or ...

A Brush with Death

by

Gerald D. Anderson

Portrait of the Artist as a Young Corpse ... or ... A Brush with Death © 2015 by Gerald D. Anderson. All rights reserved. No part of this book may be used or reproduced in any manner whatsoever, including Internet usage, without written permission from the author, except in the case of brief quotations embodied in critical articles and reviews.

First edition, 2015

ISBN-13: 978-1512009972
ISBN-10: 1-5120-0997-0

Cover design by Paul Anderson

This is a work of fiction. Names, characters, places, and incidents are either the product of the author's imagination or are used fictitiously, and any resemblance to actual persons, living or dead, business establishments, events, or locales is entirely coincidental.

OTHER BOOKS BY GERALD ANDERSON

Fiction

The Uffda Trial

Saving England

One and a Half Stone of Stories

Palmer Knutson Mystery Series:

- *Death Before Dinner*
- *Murder Under the Loon*
- *Pecked to Death ... or ... Murder Under the Prairie Chicken*
- *Murder in Bemidji ... or ... Paul's Bloody Trousers*
- *The Unicorn Murder ... or ... Victoria's Revenge*

Nonfiction

Fascists, Communists, and the National Government

Study Guide: The Western Perspective, Volumes I and II

Prairie Voices: An Oral History of Scandinavian Americans in the Upper Midwest

This book is dedicated to two wonderful sisters,

Majel Hall and Corrine Gunderson.

CHAPTER ONE

"Every one is as God made him, and often a great deal worse."

– Cervantes

Alek Kivi was an unlikeable man. He was an unpleasant, unappealing, offensive, and unattractive man. Most people experienced a visceral contempt upon meeting him, but as they really got to know him their dislike turned into loathing. If one were to bend over backward to excuse his repulsiveness, they might say, "Well, he can't help it; that's just the way he is." That might have been true, in a way, but he was, after all, the archetype of a self-made man.

He was not popular in high school, but did not engender hatred. He grew up on the Iron Range, inspired by Bobby Zimmerman of nearby Hibbing, but he was ignored every bit as much as the Bob-Dylan-to-be was. It was in college where he found his true calling, apparently striving for such titles as "least popular" and "least likely to succeed." He had been a fairly good student in high school, and when he entered Fergus Falls State University, the home of the Fergus Falls Flying Falcons, he was considering a pre-med curriculum. He signed up for the usual mélange of required and elective courses, among which were chemistry and art. He needed chemistry for his pre-med requirements, and a bored advisor, after some urging from a colleague who implored him to send students into the much underutilized art courses, advised him to take an art class. Chemistry 101 was difficult, with plenty of difficult words and confusing things like valences, but he conscientiously spent many hours of study attempting to unravel its mysteries. Fundamentals of Art, however, was less demanding of his time and did not negatively affect his social agenda. To be sure, it was not much of an agenda, but he did like spending time with the one person who was not immediately repelled by his personality, one Carol Swenson.

So he became an art major, got decent grades, took the required courses to become a secondary school teacher, and got a job teaching eighth graders. This was not a successful endeavor, and he plotted his future. No one had ever regarded him as a scholar, but he wasn't stupid, and he had a rather low cunning that would serve him well in the years to come. He scoured various small state universities in the west, thinking that a master's degree might hold some promise of future advancement. It so happened that he found a university of little distinction that had just hired a new president who was convinced that the way forward for his institution lay in graduate students. Soon, almost every department, including art, was offering a master's degree, and they would accept almost anyone. Alek Kivi was the ultimate "almost anyone," and he returned to Minnesota with a Master of Arts degree.

And yet, things did not go according to scheme. His graduate school teachers consistently noted, in their recommendations, that he demonstrated "good technique." Kivi was greatly flattered by these comments, never realizing that to compliment an artist solely on his technique was a way to avoid saying "You have no sense of composition," "You don't have any understanding of color," or "You

have no imagination or creativity whatsoever." It was akin t[o]
remarks as "You hold that pencil nicely," or "You really d[o ...]
fat girl," or "That lovely beard does a nice job of covering [...]
"You have lovely ear lobes," or "I can't understand why everybody always [...]
you're so dumb!" He was insulted that his old professors at Fergus Falls State University did not welcome him home with open arms and resented that they did not offer him a teaching position, especially after the chair had told him to his face that he had "developed a nice technique." It was painfully explained to him, however, that the rest of the faculty had a terminal degree, a Master of Fine Arts degree. He resented the fact that when the difference was pointed out to him, it was done so with a measure of glee. By this time, to the wonderment and/or disgust of many, he had actually married Carol Swenson and was the father of a girl and a boy. His wife found a steady job teaching in an elementary school, and with her money, he bought an old farmstead that came with a modernized house and a relatively sturdy shed. At last he had his own studio.

He wavered between playing the Bohemian artist and the cool sophisticate. For a time he tried to convince people that he was descended from an offshoot of the Scottish MacDuff clan. Apparently his genealogy had been inspired by a deal he had gotten on a plaid golfing hat, for everyone in his childhood neighborhood knew that he was the son of hardscrabble Finnish miners. For a time he tried to pull off the dandified look of a squire, wearing a plaid jacket and a scarf, but gradually it became a plaid flannel shirt over a faded t-shirt, accessorized with stained Levi Dockers and scuffed shoes. He let his hair grow, let his mustache grow, then he cut his hair and added a beard, then he shaved his beard, let his hair grow back, added a pony-tail and cultivated a bandito mustache. By this time, he was full-blown into his Bohemian phase. He cast off the pretentions of middle class life, such as bathing and brushing his teeth. People would just have to accept him for his art.

For the most part they didn't, but he gradually was able to make a living off it. He would go to civic festivals, centennials, street fairs, and farmer's markets, to make a dollar in any way he could. He became a reasonably acceptable caricature portraitist, with fine technique, of course, sometimes pulling down a hundred bucks an hour. He made dozens of silhouette pictures, black images on a varnished pine board, of threshing machines and haystacks. He dabbled with "fine jewelry," and when it was too cold in his shed/studio, he moved back to his kitchen table and glued rhinestones on things.

At last fortune smiled on him. While on spring break in Montana, Sherwin Williams, a painting professor at good old FFSU, attempted to ski for the first time in his life and fell down and broke both arms. Desperate to find someone who could cover the last seven weeks of courses, the chair of the art department asked Kivi to fill in. The consensus of the faculty came only after it was argued, "After all, what real harm can he do?" and, after all, his two arms did work. It was not a mutually beneficial period for the students or the teacher. For reasons that were seemingly inexplicable to the teacher, the students were not yearning to learn to paint silhouettes. Furthermore, the joke around the art department among the students was "Get busy. Here comes Kivi." "How do you know?" "I can smell him. He must be within thirty feet!" When the Fall Semester rolled around, the absent Williams had somehow become more popular than he had ever been in his life.

Perhaps from observing this totally unpalatable lump of humanity, one would expect his farm home to be a filthy hovel. It was not. His daughter, Fiona (named during his Scottish phase), was a bright and popular eighth grader, and his son, John (named by his mother), was an exceptionally talented fifth grader. His wife had become the assistant principle of Wellstone Elementary School in Fergus Falls and demonstrated a keen eye in home decoration and was developing into a gourmet cook. Presumably his children loved him, for he had shown no antisocial tendencies where they were concerned, and it was patently obvious that Carol, for reasons best known to herself, loved the lout.

But it must still be said that his self-evaluation differed dramatically from that of others. He had proved himself to be a horrible teacher, dripping venomous insults over every student's work. He had been an untrustworthy colleague, lazy and contemptuous of everyone he met. The ladies at the food service hated him. The custodians loathed him. The guy who plowed snow in the parking lot bent every effort to cover his car with snow. And yet, whether or not it was real or delusional, he considered himself to be a magnificent artist. He would brag to other members of the FFSU art department about how much money he made during the summer. His fellow artists considered it all to be a lie, or more uncomfortably, feared it might be true. Auditors at the Internal Revenue Service were impressed by the precise treatment of Carol's W-2 forms, but were inclined to accept the totals from Alek (approximately twenty percent of what he had claimed to his fellow artists) because it never made any sense, and who actually really wanted to deal with that rat's nest?

And yet, if the truth were known, he was a better known artist than any member of the FFSU faculty. His caricatures could be found in hundreds of homes. He played the role of eccentric artist at the fairs and the rubes would walk away thinking they had just met a Minnesota Picasso. He had never learned the art of producing woodcuts, but, he reasoned, copiers do the whole process better and cheaper, and before long, all of western Minnesota was awash with greeting cards featuring threshing machine silhouettes.

One fine morning in July, this unlikable, unkempt, untrustworthy, unreliable, unamusing, unfriendly, unambitious, unclean, and untalented man, unrepresentative in every way of the fine characteristics of a true Minnesotan, looked into the mirror inside of his hall closet door. He saw a forty-one-year-old man in the prime of life. He was of medium height, slender, and his generous supply of unwashed hair had not yet begun to sprout silver threads among the mouse brown. He somehow thought the fat tissue upon which his eyebrows perched gave him a manly look (less kind people might have agreed with this, but their term would have been Cro-Magnon manliness). He ran his hand over his five-day stubble and, inexplicitly, pronounced himself satisfied. He bent down to pull on his sandals, which he referred to as his "Mexican Tiger paws." He adjusted his khaki cargo shorts, liberally smeared with paint, a new color of which he added for effect on those rare occasions when he actually did use his paints. He admired his T-shirt, which proclaimed "Nebraska Iron Man Competition, 1999." In truth, he had found the shirt at a garage sale, but he reasoned, correctly, that few Minnesotans would ever be conversant with the identities of Nebraska Iron Man competitors. He looked out across the startlingly gorgeous acres of green corn, but to no avail, because his dark brown eyes had never been able to discern pure beauty. He stepped outside and breathed in the fresh air as he walked to the mailbox. As he had expected, he found a letter addressed to him. He read the return address: "Lake Region Arts Council." His continence broke out into a smile of triumph; well, if one were to be honest, he smirked.

CHAPTER TWO

"A person's a person, no matter how small."

– Dr. Seuss

The Saturday before Memorial Day was the first decent day of spring. March had been like the middle of winter, April was lousy, and May was just as bad. In fact, the ice had finally gone off the lakes in Northwestern Minnesota only about three weeks earlier, fully a month behind normal. But this day was the one everyone had been waiting for. Cottage owners from the Twin Cities, Fargo/Moorhead, and even Winnipeg were there to open their lakeside retreats for yet another season. Scott V. Askelund and his wife Colleen, along with their little daughter Leah, who lived in a lovely home in Fargo, had arrived at Lake Lida the night before and had worked most of the morning to air out and clean their small cabin. Scott had braved the icy waters to put in the dock, and as the sun warmed them for the first time in seven months, they all went for a ride in their small fishing boat.

All of this was wonderful, but by two o'clock they were back in the cabin and Leah said, "Daddy, I'm bored."

The exasperated daddy said, "Oh come on, Leah, we've only been out here for one day. Go throw some rocks in the lake."

"I don't wanna throw rocks in the lake," the little girl said. "I want to go to the flea market!"

Scott thought for a minute and decided that it did sound like more fun than spending the rest of the day with a whiny kid. He yelled out to Colleen who was sunning herself on the dock: "Hey Colleen, how about going to the Detroit Lakes flea market?"

"What, now?"

"Sure, that's always fun. Let's go."

Colleen flexed her shoulders, enjoying the warmth of the sun and said, "No, why don't you just take Leah."

Of course, by this time Leah was all excited to go and Scott could not get out of it, but then, he had always liked to browse around and look at the unusual stuff for sale. Maybe he would even buy one of those antique ice-fishing lures for the growing collection that was perched, so to speak, on the shelf above the door. *Who knows?* he thought, *Perhaps this will be the beginning of a swell father/daughter tradition.*

There was a wonderful crowd at the Shady Acres flea market, and the people seemed to be walking around with the spirit of cows that have been kept in the barn all winter, only to be freed to graze on the fresh green grass. Scott and Leah wondered among the trees, which had only recently sprouted leaves, and Scott slowed down as he walked by "rustic antiques," where he overheard an elderly man proclaim, "Twenty bucks for an old horse collar? Hell, I just threw out five of them there things that were in the barn, and they were in much better shape than that!" They walked quickly by a tent of glass collectables, used books, old records in their original album covers, used sporting equipment, and a large tent full of sweatshirts, some appliqued in pastels and others that contained messages from the cute ("Grandchildren are wonderful") to the bizarre ("Friends help you move, good friends help you move bodies!"). This did not interest them, but they soon found several tables featuring a huge collection of toys that were not old enough to be antiques, but old enough to engender the spirit of nostalgia for any adult who had had a happy childhood. Leah was mesmerized by the vintage Barbie Dolls, but Scott remembered Colleen making some comment that she was determined to keep those "grotesquely misshaped dolls" out of Leah's hands. Instead, he bought her a large *Disney Princesses Coloring Book*, with Snow White, Cinderella, Beauty, etc., just to have on hand for a rainy day at the lake. Leah was into princesses, and often walked around the house with a veil and a wand.

Scott kicked around a used tool display, and led a bored Leah around a small classic car exhibit. At the fishing equipment tent, he found an old wooden perch that would be used as an ice fishing lure and bought it for a couple of bucks. They enjoyed ice cream cones and later shared a can of pop. *This is fun*, thought Scott. *I've got to take my little girl out just by ourselves more often, before she turns into a teenager.*

This thought occurred to him as he saw a pouty-lipped, indecently clad teenage girl posing for a caricature. They walked over to watch the artist at work. A sign reading "Portraits by Alek" adorned a small tent, in front of which the artist himself plied his craft. Scott looked at the caricature and at the pouty-lipped adolescent and noted a vague resemblance. "Oh Daddy, Daddy, can I have my picture done? Please? Please?" Scott relied on the tried-and-true method of dealing with such pleas by saying, "Perhaps, but not today. I know Mommy should be here so she can comb your hear to make you look like a real princess. Daddy doesn't know how to do that." In any event, judging by the guy's talent, he might not be here much longer. Inside the tent he noticed a series of varnished boards with farm scene silhouettes and wondered *Who the hell would ever buy anything like that?* just as two women began to fight over one, each claiming to have found it first. The artist excused himself, found another board that was for all practical purposes a clone of the first, and settled the matter for the two, now happy, women. Scott looked at the price and winced.

Leah, meanwhile, had discovered a table of "handmade original jewelry" and had found a ring that looked just like the one that Rapunzel was wearing in her new book. "Oh look, Daddy! There's Rapunzel's ring. Just like Rapunzel's ring! Will you buy me Rapunzel's ring Daddy? Please Daddy?" Scott looked at the picture in the book, and questioned just how "original" the artist's jewelry was. No doubt he had a daughter in his home. It was just a large rhinestone stuck on a silver colored band, but, well, maybe it would be a nice memento of the day at the flea market. He remembered that he kept stuff he had gotten at the county fair for years. It was only ten bucks, but he talked the artist down to eight. Everybody, but mostly Leah, was happy, and after hearing her say "I can hardly wait to show it to Mommy," it was a golden opportunity to leave.

Leah eagerly rushed into the cabin to show her mother the new ring. Colleen rolled her eyes at Scott and mouthed the words "spoiling the kid," but she enjoyed seeing how happy Leah was with her Rapunzel treasure. She would not take off the ring even when she went to bed.

The next day was not quite as warm, but everyone looked forward to Memorial Day, when the forecast was for highs in the low eighties. The whole family sat on the dock and fished for perch, bluegills, and sunfish, throwing almost all of them back but keeping a few to fry for supper. Leah, who had been so excited to go fishing, however, had become quiet and looked quite sad. It was then that Colleen noticed that, although the sun was glinting off the water, it was no longer glinting off Leah's finger.

"What happened to your ring, Sweetheart?"

"I lost the pretty stone."

"Where did you lose it? I'll help you look for it."

"I don't know. I don't wanna look for it anyway."

Well, there's eight bucks I could just as well have thrown into the lake! thought Scott. Aloud he said, "May I see your ring, Princess?" On observing it, he said, "Look, the whole part that held the stone broke off. It is now just a silver band, so it's no longer like Rapunzel's engagement ring, it's like her wedding ring after she married the Prince. I think that's even better!" He looked over at Colleen and she mouthed, "Brilliant!"

Leah was happy again, but not for long. By late afternoon she was complaining that her tummy hurt. By suppertime she was crying, and by eight o'clock she was starting to scream. Scott and Colleen wasted little time in packing things up and sped Leah to the hospital emergency room in Fargo. In a remarkably short time, a doctor was able to examine the little girl. The parents had to admit that he appeared to be a very skilled young doctor. He was able to calm down Leah, and even though she was still in pain she was able to talk to him. He asked her if she had eaten any unusual plants or things that she found near the lake, she was able to tell him that she had not, saying that she hadn't even been able to eat the little fishies that she had caught. He tried again, and asked her if she had swallowed anything else. Leah was very quiet, then finally nodded her head and started to cry.

"What is it Leah? What did you swallow?" the doctor asked gently.

"I swallowed my diamond!" she wailed.

The doctor gave a questioning look to the parents, and Scott hurriedly explained, "I bought her a ring at the Detroit Lakes Flea Market yesterday, she called it her Rapunzel ring. She is still wearing the ... um ... ring part of the ring. Why didn't you tell us you had swallowed the diamond, Leah?"

"I was too embarrassed," she bawled.

The young doctor smiled at the big word from the little mouth and said, "Will you show me your ring, Leah?"

Leah took it off and handed it to the doctor, who examined it under a bright light. Turning to Scott, he asked, "How large was this diamond?"

"I donno, kind of hard to say. I suppose it was the size of a bean. Won't that just pass through? Why should that give her such a stomach ache?"

"The stone might very well pass. The first thing I will try will be to give her a rather strong version of a laxative. I fear, however, that that is not the problem. We may have a very sick little girl here."

"What! What do you mean?" Colleen gasped.

"I can't know for sure—I will have to send this ring to the lab to see if there are enough particles remaining from where the 'diamond' setting was affixed so that tests can be made—but I suspect that she may be suffering from lead poisoning. Most jewelry makers use a special kind of solder, the kind of solder that will 'essay,' as they say. Lead is not used in this professional type of solder alloy. The kind of solder one uses at home to fix a toaster or something is ordinary cheap coil solder and contains a lot of lead and tin. I suspect that this just what the jewelry maker used—totally irresponsibly, I might say. From the symptoms of acute abdominal pain, I suspect that we may have a case of lead poisoning."

"But isn't that what kids who live in the slums get from the paint? That's supposed to take a long time before anybody even knows about it. That's why lead paint has been banned for years."

"Exactly, but if a large chunk of lead is ingested at one time, especially by a small child, the results could be very, very serious."

"Fatal?" Colleen gasped.

The doctor nodded grimly and said, "It has happened, yes, but in this case I am hopeful that you have gotten her to the hospital in time. I am immediately ordering a hospital room and we will start the purging process as soon as possible. If we are unable to get the stone and the setting out by purging, we may have to resort to surgery to remove it. Will you be able to stay with her? I think she will need her parents before this night is over. "

Scott gritted his teeth and said, "Just try to keep us out!" Already, however, he was thinking of that smarmy artist who had done this to his little girl.

CHAPTER THREE

"Home cooking. Where many a man thinks his wife is."

– Jimmy Durante

It was a quiet Tuesday night in June in Fergus Falls. The weekend cabin owners had mostly gone back to Fargo or the Twin Cities. The resorts were filled with contented people who wished to stay for the long twilight. The bars and restaurants of the area had sparse attendance, and there was little for the deputies of the sheriff's department do to. Chief Deputy Orly Peterson had scheduled a minimum presence of personnel and had sent the rest home to their families. Peterson stayed in his office, however, because he was in charge. Sheriff Palmer Knutson was off on a trip to Norway, tracking down relatives and absorbing the nature of his roots. Peterson had promised his wife Allysha, ten weeks away from bringing another Swedish-American into the world, that he would be home be home before eight. It was now a quarter to nine. He had never realized just how much tedious paperwork went with the job of being sheriff.

When his telephone rang, he was just about to tell his wife that he would be home in ten minutes. Instead, he was informed that a 911 call had been received concerning a domestic dispute. The dispatcher informed him that there was a life-threatening situation at the home of William Bjerke, north of Fergus Falls on

Highway 59. The call was relayed to him and simply said, "This is Betty Bjerke, on the Erhard road. My husband is trying to kill me."

Peterson looked around, then checked the roster. There was really nobody else he could send, or at least who could be trusted to handle the situation. He sighed, made a quick call to Allysha to tell her that he would be much later than he anticipated, and reported his destination to the main desk. He took two steps toward the door, then went back to retrieve his Glock. He hated domestic situations. They were always unpleasant and were sometimes dangerous, and sometimes it was better to be armed. He climbed into his sheriff's department vehicle, adorned with an incredible array of lights and more decorations than a Hapsburg Empire royal coach. As he did so, he thought, *William Bjerke? Willian Bjerke? My God, that's Wild Bill!* To be sure, "Wild Bill" had never been charged with a felony, but the number of his DUI charges was legendary, his game violations were infamous, and his petty theft charges and complaints about him from neighbors and from the pollution control agency were all too frequent. Peterson could picture the trashy dump just a mile or so north off the Interstate. "You'll owe me on this one, Palmer," Orly muttered.

Peterson put on his siren and raced up Interstate 94 until he reached exit 50. In about a minute he came to a depressing house, devoid of paint and surrounded by three dead cars and a rusty pickup. With the lights flashing, he got out of his car and advanced to the front door. His hand went to his Glock as a mangy dog, of indeterminate breed, came barking and snarling toward him. He would never willing shoot a dog, but if he had to, this was just the kind that was asking to be shot. The mangy cur's bark might have been worse than his bite, but Peterson was not anxious to compare them. Still, in a domestic violence situation, the last thing an officer should do is to start blasting away. He tried a combination of soothing words and walking with authority until he reached the front porch, a groaning rickety thing badly in need of paint. He knocked on the door. "Sheriff's office! We've had an emergency call from this address. Open up!"

Peterson was greeted by a blast of beer odor as the door was jerked open and a drunk, balding, rat-faced man in an undershirt that strained to hold in fifty extra pounds of pure fat answered the door. "I didn't call you!"

"I don't expect you did," Peterson replied, "but someone at this address called 911. Where is your wife, sir?"

"Sir! It's not every day that someone calls me that! What do you want Betty for?" Bjerke stood in the doorway blocking entry.

Determined to take control of the situation, Peterson politely inquired, "Is there anyone else besides you and Mrs. Bjerke who reside at this address?"

A slurred voice demanded, "What's it to you?"

Ignoring the question, Peterson forced his head in and called, "Mrs. Bjerke, this is Chief Deputy Peterson of the Otter Tail County Sheriff's Department. Are you all right?"

When he heard a faint whimper, Peterson put his hand on several inches of fat and shoved Bjerke aside. Betty Bjerke was curled up on a dingy out-of-date sofa with her hands covering her face. With a stern and contemptuous look at "Wild Bill," Peterson knelt before Betty Bjerke and assured her that "Everything is all right now. He won't hurt you anymore." He gently brushed some hair from her face and noticed what would soon be a black eye glowing on the left side of her face.

"Sit down," he ordered Wild Bill, who obeyed immediately, plopping himself down on an aged and stained La-Z-Boy recliner. Peterson noticed the subdued and gloomy expression on his face. Turning to Betty, he asked, "Are you hurt anyplace other than your face? Should I call an ambulance?" Betty shook her head indicating a negative response to both questions.

"Feel like a big man, hitting a little woman, do you?" he roared out at Wild Bill. Bill stared down at the floor. An old fashioned clock on a shelf ticked during a long moment of silence. The deputy finally turned to Betty and asked, "Has he hit you before?"

Tears dripped from her eyes as she silently nodded.

"Often?"

"No," Betty whispered, "but maybe I deserved it this time."

"Nobody ever deserves it, Mrs. Bjerke." Turning to Wild Bill he lowered his voice and asked, "Why don't you tell me just what happened here."

Sobering up rapidly, Bill said, "Well, maybe you're right, she maybe didn't deserve to get hit, and she's right, I have lost my temper and hit her a couple of times over the last fifteen years when I have had a few too many brewskies, but not lately."

"So why now?" Orly calmly asked.

Bill gave a somewhat embarrassed glance at his wife and said, "I was just sitting having a few beers with a couple of other guys at Ralph's Bar when Eddie Ryan came in and told me that he had just stopped by Mabel Murphy's to pick up his daughter—she's a high school kid who has an after-school job there. He asks me all innocent-like who Betty's new boyfriend is, like it is a joke that I must be in on. He said she was sharing a glass of wine with this here longhaired guy and they were sitting in a booth. A booth, mind you! I came straight home and was waiting for her when she dragged in long after we should have been having supper. At first, she denied everything, saying Eddie must have been mistaken, but I could tell she was lying." A thunderous belch followed. "Nothing like this had ever happened before—for either of us, I might add—and I demanded she tell me who it was. She refused, denying she was even in Mabel Murphy's, and I lost my temper and I let her have it. Well, then she fessed up and told me the truth. I could hardly believe her when she said who it was, but I guess I made some sorta rash threat to get my shotgun and go after the son-of-a-bitch and would take care of her while I was at it. That was when she called 911."

Orly turned to Betty and sympathetically asked, "Is that pretty much the way it was?"

Betty let out a wail and sobbed openly as the tears gushed out of her shining face. "Yes, yes, it was all my fault."

The deputy held her hand with compassion, looked her in the good eye and said, "No, Betty, it was not all your fault. You did not use physical violence, Bill did."

"But I drove him to it," she sobbed. "We had met this guy at that flea market south of Detroit Lakes a couple of weeks ago. He made these lovely painted boards and he made jewelry, and he was ever so clever. He drew pictures of people and they really were not very expensive at all. Bill was off someplace looking at gopher traps or something and I decided to surprise him by having my picture done for his birthday present next week."

"Aw, Betty, why didn't you tell me?" croaked Wild Bill.

"I just said, it was supposed to be a surprise," she sobbed. "Anyway, he was real nice and we talked quite a while and he said he lived not too far from us and he asked me all sorts of questions about what I did and what I thought of things and talked to me like nobody else had done for years."

"Ah, Betty."

"But then somebody else came up and wanted their picture done and he said that he had enjoyed talking to me and that maybe we could talk again sometime and then he held my hand and I told him my number was in the book and then he said he would call and I told him not to but I sort of wished he would and then he called this afternoon and said that he was at Mabel Murphy's and that he would like if I could join him for a glass of wine. Nobody has offered me a glass of wine in a dozen years!" More tears rained down.

Deputy Peterson put his little finger in Bjerke's left nostril and led him over to a corner of the room. "All right, Wild Bill, if I were you I would get down on my knees in front of your wife and beg her forgiveness. A little tenderness and comforting is just what is called for here, and maybe even a nice cup of tea—you can boil water, can't you? And maybe while you're at it, some coffee might help sober you up. Remember that every time anyone is called out on a 911 emergency, there has to be a report. I could have you in jail tonight on a charge of battery and being a public nuisance. I am extremely reluctant to leave Betty alone with someone who has just assaulted her. Sure, you say you are sorry now, but what assurance do I have that you won't hit her again the moment I leave?"

"I won't, I promise. Ask Betty, she knows I'll never do it again, don't you Betty?"

Betty sniffed and wiped back a new tear and said, "I guess I know William"—at the sound of *William*, Bill's face sagged—"better than anyone on earth. I am sure he will behave himself. If, for some reason, he doesn't, I can call you again, can't I, Mr. Peterson?"

"Absolutely, Betty. Day or night," Orly said. To Bill, he added, "Remember, there will be a record of this, and if anybody from the sheriff's office has to come out here again because you have been beating your wife, well, you will wish for a very long time that you hadn't done it. Do I make myself clear?"

Wild Bill, perhaps out of habit, mumbled, "Yes, your honor."

"What?"

"I mean, yes, Mister Peterson."

CHAPTER FOUR

"By trying, we can easily learn to endure adversity.

Another man's, I mean."

– Mark Twain

Business had been exceptionally good at Alek Kivi's tent for the first days of the Otter Tail County Fair. The number of vain mothers with homely kids and the incredible hopes of teenage girls that their faces could always look better than they did in a mirror never ceased to be a goldmine. He had quickly learned to ignore the weak chin and the buck teeth or the shifty eyes to present each patron with whatever positive trait that could be found, however superficially. To be sure, he had had to make some changes to his jewelry line. The episode with a public health official and that guy threatening him with everything from a lawsuit to great bodily harm had convinced him to discontinue his soldered ring line, but it was easy enough to switch. The "Native American Collection" was, if anything, making even more money. He used safe feathers and beads. In light of the near disaster of that little girl, he had even gone so far as to check that the beads were nontoxic and would not present a great risk if swallowed. In his workshop he could turn out beaded rings and bracelets, and necklaces made of a leather shoelace decorated with pheasant feathers, items that turned a better profit per hour of labor than theater popcorn. He *suggested* that everything was based on traditional "Native American Designs," and rather resented the comment of one shopper who informed him that "You wouldn't know Native American design if it jumped up and bit you on the ass!" The farm silhouettes were selling as well as ever.

In the late afternoon of the final day of the fair, he had just achieved the near impossible by doing a caricature of a pathetically homely girl and making her look cute, when he looked into the tent to see a chubby, gray-haired bespeckled man holding what looked to be a pair of calipers to one of his silhouettes. He measured the house, jotted something down in a notebook, and took out a drafting compass. Kivi walked over to him and attempted to be friendly, saying, "Hello there. Nice day, huh? Have you found something you like?"

"Yes, yes, I certainly have," the man replied, in a tone that almost seemed threatening.

In his oiliest manner, Kivi said, "Ah yes, one of my 'Harvest Time' selections. What do you like about it?"

"I like the house. The reason I like the house is that it is my house."

"Wonderful. It always makes it special when we see a picture that perfectly matches our memory of home, isn't it?"

"I don't need a memory of my home. I still live there. That is my house!"

"Yes, I hear that a lot. It makes me very happy to know that people see that house and it brings them happiness."

"It doesn't bring me happiness. It brings me to contemplate a lawsuit."

A startled Kivi sputtered, "What, um … what do you mean?"

The stranger moved uncomfortably close to Kivi and said, "Obviously this silhouette is based on a photograph of a house located west of Pelican Rapids. Do you deny that you used a photograph of a real house as the basis for your so-called art?"

"Well, I use several aids in producing my art. I suppose I may have used a photograph as the basis for this house, but you can't seriously claim that it is exclusively your house."

The stranger gave a Kivi a rather malicious grin and said, "As a matter of fact, I can. You see, that is not just an ordinary farm house. I designed and built it myself. My name is Emil Holte, and I am a professor of architecture at North Dakota State University. I have long been fascinated in what is called the 'Golden Mean.' Now, in mathematical terms, this may sound simple, two quantities are in the 'golden ratio' if their ratio is the same as the sum of the larger of the two quantities. This 'divine proportion,' or 'golden proportion,' has been around since the time of Pythagoras and Euclid. In a golden rectangle, for instance, the rectangle can be cut into a square and a smaller rectangle with the same aspect ratio. It is immutable. But there is more."

Shifting into a pretentious professorial mode, the man went on to say, "It is not just mathematicians who use the Golden Mean. For centuries, artists, historians, psychologists, biologists—and yes, architects—have been fascinated with its perfection. I refer, of course, to the great Le Corbusier. It is found throughout nature—in plants, animals, and human anatomy. Consider the perfection of the spiral that is found in the nautilus. It has, I am convinced, played a role in the very perception of humanity. Surely, as an artist, you must be familiar with this."

Kivi frantically tried to remember something from one of his graduate courses, but since his teacher didn't understand it very well, it was somewhat swept under the rug. Trying to brazen it out, he said, indignantly, "Well, of course, but what does that have to do with this house?"

"What? Did you not notice that it was far more perfect than an average farm house? I spent years incorporating the Golden Mean into the design of that most American of all institutions, the farm house. That house employs the Golden Mean in every inch of its design and construction. I have received multiple national—and international, I might add—awards for that house. It has been featured in several architectural textbooks. One is welcome to photograph the house, I have no problem with that, but by using it in a commercial endeavor, you are breaking all sorts of intellectual copyright laws. I must demand satisfaction." Holte wasn't at all sure this was true, but he was positive Kivi wouldn't know one way or the other.

Kivi was losing patience with somebody who seemed to be some kind of intellectual windbag. "Yeah, yeah, yeah. So prove it!"

"What do you think I was doing with my compass and calipers? One of my students just happened to pass by your pathetic tent, and, somewhat amused, he stopped in and saw your silhouettes. He recognized it right away—as most students of architecture would. I must insist that you cease selling these … er … things, and I demand an accounting of all of them that have been sold already."

"Insist all you want, and then go take a long walk off a short dock!"

"Have no doubt, I shall be turning this matter over to my attorney!"

Kivi noticed someone standing by his easel looking like a potential caricature customer. "Yeah, you do that. In the meantime, put an egg in your shoe and beat it."

Holte put his face within three inches of Kivi's smug countenance and said, "I might add, you insignificant philistine, that after consulting with my attorney, I just may come back and take it out of your hide." With that note of defiance, he executed a heroic about-face and strode off.

Kivi watched him go and turned to his potential customer. The man held up a caricature that he had just completed two hours earlier. "You the guy who did this picture of my daughter?"

"Yeah. How do you like it?"

In answer to this question, the man made a fist and hit Kivi on the nose. He fell flat on his ass. It had not been a good day.

CHAPTER FIVE

"Painting: The art of protecting flat surfaces from the weather and exposing them to the critic."

– Ambrose Bierce

On a warm evening on the third of July, the nine-member board of the Lake Region Arts Council was meeting at its headquarters in the River Inn building in downtown Fergus Falls. For fifty years, this had been the finest hotel in the area. It had opened in 1929, shortly before the nation was plunged into the Great Depression. Ironically, the reason the hotel had been built in the first place helped to sustain it during the desperate thirties. It was located across the street from the United States District Court building so that judges and well-heeled lawyers would have an appropriately posh place to stay. During the Depression era, there were countless bankruptcy hearings, eviction hearings, lawsuits, and new federal programs that kept the court building, hence the River Inn, rather full. To be sure, the price of a room, and a cup of coffee in the delightful coffee shop, had to be reduced, but compared to almost any other business in town, the River Inn did all right.

As well it should have! The lobby featured rich paneling, a wood-beamed ceiling, a beautiful floor, and offered comfortable seating. The rooms were spacious for the times and many were equipped with a small balcony. But times change. Interstate 94 was almost two miles away and the hotels that sprouted up by exit 54 began to appeal more to the modern traveler. The building was structurally sound, however, and had been well maintained, so it was eventually made into apartments and commercial space. The Lake Region Arts Council managed to acquire the best space of all.

The Lake Region Arts Council represents nine counties in West Central Minnesota, and all nine board members were gathered to deal with an emergency situation. The artist who had been scheduled for a showing of her exquisite woodcuts had abruptly canceled the entire event because she had been offered a chance to show her work in an exhibition organized by the Danish government. The Council could hardly blame her, because the opportunity to show her work in her home city of Copenhagen was a lifelong dream. But still, it did put them in somewhat of a bind. The council met in the spacious office of Harriet Monroe, the executive director. The office had once been the luxurious dining hall of the River Inn, and featured glass doors that opened to balconies overlooking the river and the old Otter Tail Power Company dam.

Acknowledging that every board member was present, she called the meeting to order. "As you know, the purpose of this meeting tonight is to decide what we should do as a result of Sonja Danielsen's sudden decision to cancel her exhibit, which was to open in only five weeks' time. Those of you who read the article in the *Journal* or the *Fargo Forum* can appreciate the difficulties that we now face. I must add that there was a quite wonderful article in the *Minneapolis Star Tribune* that not only highlighted our problem, but also went out of its way to extol the whole arts scene in Fergus Falls. In one sense, this almost increases the problem, because we have a lot to live up to, and the idea of leaving the gallery empty during the August and September period, when we still have a lot of tourists around, does not sound appealing. Basically, the question is, 'What shall we do?'"

At first, the board members were somewhat hesitant to speak up, but for a while the consensus seemed to be that there would be no great harm in cancelling the late summer show. One of the members asked for the opinion of the executive director. Ms. Monroe replied, "I took the liberty of contacting a few regional artists to see if any of them were prepared to step in at a moment's notice. I have not contacted those who have recently shown their work at the Lake Region Arts gallery or in Fargo-Moorhead or Alexandria. One of the artists I had in mind has just opened an exhibition in that nice little gallery in Wahpeton, so he's out. I contacted Wallace Duncan at Fergus Falls State University, but most of the arts faculty were gone this summer and would not be back in time to set up a show. I got the same result from the chairs of the art departments at Minnesota State University Moorhead, Concordia College, and NDSU. St. Cloud State has not returned my calls. Now, of course, this represents only the academic portion of local artists, and I realize that that there are many independent artists who would be able to provide us with a unique show. So far, however, I have yet to find one who has a portfolio ready to go at a minute's notice. I can't blame them, because one should have at least a year to plan their exhibition. Any thoughts?"

The member from Douglas County said, "There was a nice exhibit in Alexandria that just closed last month. Is that too close?"

Ms. Monroe replied. "Yes. I think it is. Definitely. Besides, this is a regional arts organization, and if we are to have a showing, I think it is incumbent upon us to offer new experiences in art."

The member from Becker County said, "There was a watercolor show in Detroit Lakes this spring. Would there be any interest in something like that?"

"I suppose there would, but a show like that is not that much different from the arts and crafts tent at a county fair. I mean, you can find a nice picture or two, but the artist usually never has a real portfolio of work. And if one wants to include an entire show, one ends up with a lot of, let's face it, really bad stuff. Our purpose must be to show fine art, or at least, art that is challenging, unusual, or uniquely representative of our region."

Bertram Flom had been silent during this discussion. Flom did not really know that much about art, but he liked being a board member of anything. He had worked hard to achieve his lofty place in the Fergus Falls business circle, but the most effective thing he had ever done was to be born to the founder of Flom Home Appliances. He had been an unimpressive student at Fergus Falls State University, but nobody really cared, certainly not himself, because his future was assured. About the best thing that could be said about his business acumen would be to note that he had "kept it going." He maintained a certain lifestyle befitting a "business executive," moving his family into his father's huge house on Court Street. He belonged to the local Lion's Club, he made "often enough" appearances at his local church, and he sponsored events for the Boy Scouts and the high school athletic teams. He was a tall, still-athletic, handsome man, with blue eyes and distinguished wisps of gray in the temples of his light brown hair. By and large, everybody seemed to like Bert, but when he attempted turn what he considered popularity into a bid for the Republican Party nomination for the state legislature, he failed spectacularly. The truth was that many people identified with his mediocrity, and basically respected him for it. His wife, Cynthia, however, thought it would be nice to attend arts events, so he had managed to become one of the members of the board of the Lake Region Arts Council. Other than helping rid meetings of coffee and doughnuts, he had contributed little. But now, he opened his mouth, saying, "I have an idea."

The other board members, somewhat astounded at this hitherto unsaid part of Bert's vocabulary, turned to look at him. "I think," he said, "that we have relied too much on hoity-toity college teachers for our exhibitions. I mean, they do make wonderful art, don't get me wrong, but I think we should have an ordinary artist once in a while."

The Clay County member asked, "An ordinary artist. I thought the whole point was to encourage something just a bit above that particular creative milestone."

"Well, see," Flom continued, "that's what we have always done. Most of the people in our region do not go to see the art shows at FFSU, or MSUM or Concordia or our fine gallery right here. Now, of course, I would argue that they should. But we all know they don't. Where do most of them see their yearly quota of art? The see it at the county fairs or some of those summer arts and crafts fairs."

Another member piped up with "I think you got a point there, Bert, but what are you suggesting?"

"I think we should try to find a 'People's Artist,' one who is well known to the public and whose art is affordable and purchased by the public. I think it would be a wonderful public relations move on our part, and if we get plenty of people in for, er, this artist's show, well, then they would be more likely to come to other shows."

Ms. Monroe opened her mouth to protest but at that moment another representative said, "You know, Bert, that's not too stupid."

"Thank you," said Bert.

"But do you have anybody in mind?"

Bert squirmed in his chair. "Well, no. I mean, I don't know enough about art to make that kind of recommendation." At this announcement, at least five heads nodded in grim agreement. "But I keep seeing this one artist almost everywhere I go. There always seem to be a lot of people hanging around his tent, and I know that his work hangs in a lot of homes around here."

"And who might this be?" asked the Clay County member testily.

"It's that there Finnish fellow. I think his name is Alex, no, Alek Kivi. You must have seen him. I talked to him a little bit last summer, and he told me that he even taught at good old Fergus Falls State for a bit."

"I know that guy," said an enthusiastic member, warming to the challenge. "We got one of his silhouette paintings hanging in our living room."

Ms. Monroe looked at him and began to mentally compose her letter of resignation, while the Clay County member just stared with his mouth hanging open. The member from Grant County then asked, "What other kind of work does he do?"

"Oh, he does lots of stuff," Flom said, apparently getting excited over his idea. "He paints these quick pictures of people, sort of like cartoons."

"Do you mean caricatures?" the executive director asked.

"Yeah, that's it. Caricatures! And he makes this really neat jewelry, too. I'm sure he could fill the gallery space."

"Well, so could three Herefords and a couple of sheep. That's hardly a criterion!" said the member from Douglas County.

"I don't know," the member from Clay County said. "Perhaps if the animals had been shown at the fair, after all. Look, you can't be serious, Bert. The reputation of the Lake Region Arts Council is at stake here. If this is the guy I'm thinking it might be, well, he does have a reputation, but it is a reputation earned from a few weeks teaching at Fergus Falls State. As you know, I've got a lot of artists in my county, and I go to a few events at the colleges and I hear them talk. I once heard them guffawing after a gallery talk and I asked what was so funny. They finally told me they were telling the latest Kivi stories from Fergus Falls. This would not go over well with those folks. I'm afraid it is just impossible."

But the member who had just attested that his art collection included a Kivi silhouette looked offended. "Well, I don't know about his reputation, but you can say a lot of nasty things about most artists, in my experience. The whole point of art is to appreciate it for what it is, and, dammit, Gale and I love out farm scene. I think we should vote on it!"

Omigod, thought the executive director. *This could actually go through!*

A few enthusiastic members nodded to the vote suggestion, and only a few seconds later a vote had been taken. By a vote of six to three, it was decided that Alek Kivi should be invited to exhibit his art in the River Inn gallery in five weeks' time. The three dissenting voters huddled briefly and agreed to reconvene at Mabel Murphy's for some medicine in a shot glass.

CHAPTER SIX

"A thousand words will not leave so deep an impression as one deed."

– Henrik Ibsen

It was the second week of August and Sheriff Palmer Knutson had just returned from his long vacation trip to Scandinavia. He had seen no point in getting to his office early, and had given himself plenty of time to catch up on the news from the Vikings' training camp, the dismal standings of the Twins, Timberwolves trade rumors, and what had happened in all of his favorite comics. The other news he had been able to keep up on during his travels, due to Ellie's iPad. Fortified by two cups of coffee, Palmer felt content to climb behind the wheel of his Acura and make his way to the Otter Tail County Courthouse. He gazed with affection at the flowers surrounding the courthouse, at the Ionic pillars, and at the eagle over the door. He appreciated the immediate effect of the air conditioning as he made his way across the eight-pointed star on the main floor and gazed again at the painting depicting the aftermath of the 1919 tornado. He smiled as he spotted the otters on the molded brass doorknobs. He looked affectionately at his brass doorplate and opened his door to gaze unaffectionately at his computer. He sat down on his special leather swivel chair and looked around him. Everything was as he remembered it. The flags of the United States and the State of Minnesota still guarded the sides of his desk, his large maps of Minnesota and Otter Tail County still covered the back wall, and his wolf skin, complete with a head full of snarling teeth (or "that hideous thing" as Ellie called it) still hung in its place of honor. Now that he had been to Norway the Hardanger lace that covered his oak credenza seemed extra special. He reckoned that he ought to go in to see his chief deputy, Orly Peterson, to get caught up on the last three weeks, but that could wait. Perhaps just a bit more coffee….

"Hey Palmer, welcome back," bellowed Deputy Peterson, knocking and entering at the same time. "Yer lookin' good!"

Knutson, who had spent a dreary minute in the bathroom before he left home, staring at his greying dark blonde hair, receding ever so inevitably, his light blue eyes, now covered by bi-focals, and his waistline that took up one more notch in his belt than it had before his vacation, did not want to argue with Orly, so he merely said, "Thank you, and so are you." This was not a lie. Peterson, as usual, had on his spotless, precisely pressed tan uniform, with the brown epaulettes supported by his manly shoulders and his gold O.T.C.S.D (Otter Tail County Sheriff's Department) pin glowing in the sun. The utter perfection of this Swede made Palmer tired.

"So, did you have a good time in Norway?" Orly asked with somewhat of a smirk.

"Well, yes," Palmer allowed, "and we had a nice three days in Iceland, and about ten days in Sweden."

With a rather mischievous glint in his eye, Peterson said, "I believe you said you were going to rent a car over there. How did that turn out?"

"Um, fine. We didn't rent a car in Iceland, but we did in Norway and Sweden. They have generally good roads over there, especially in Sweden. We saw a lot of Saabs and Volvos, as you might expect, and in Sweden we actually saw a few American cars."

"So, no trouble at all, huh?"

"Not really, no."

Peterson pretended to think deeply and then said, "That's interesting, because one morning I had an interesting call from a judge in Norway."

Oh God, no! Palmer thought.

"It seems," the deputy slowly said, "that the Norwegian highway police had stopped an American whom they claimed had put the lives of their citizens in considerable danger. They called me to see if I could provide them with any information on the man."

I can't believe it! Those supercilious a-holes! thought Knutson.

"I'm sure there is a story here. You might as well tell me now."

"Oh, all right. Well, Ellie and I had rented a car. We were able to enjoy that in the south of Norway, going all the way down to Grimstad. That's where Ibsen came from, not that he spent much time in the old home town. Anyhow, that is right on the ocean, and it is so beautiful that it just makes your eyes hurt. Well, then we drove up and did Oslo, the Royal Palace, Frogner Park, and all the tourist things. It was all fairly easy, and, as I said, Sweden was just a treat for traveling. So, it was getting toward the end of our time, and we had decided to go up north, to where the old ancestral place was. I had tracked down some shirt-tail relatives and we had exchanged e-mails, and they asked us to come up and stay with them. I gotta admit, we were rather counting on this, because everything in that country is unbelievably expensive. So here we are, coming from southern Sweden and we get into Norway and go around Oslo, and I'm kind of proud of myself for doing this because it is getting to be the rush hour. About twenty miles north of Oslo, I needed gas, so I took an exit off the freeway—one of the few areas that has four-lane highways—and bought some gas. Uffda! One might think what with all those off-shore oil rigs one could get gas a little cheaper. No so. It was almost three times as high as in America. Well, anyway, I got back in and was about to leave when Ellie said she wanted to fill up the water bottle.

"Now here I have to stop to tell you something that really bites my hinder." At this, Orly had to suppress a grin. Palmer's continual effort to avoid using uncouth words was always amusing. "So here we are, in Norway. What do they have in Norway? They got mountains—mountains up the wazoo! What comes out of mountains? Mountain streams! They've got as much fresh, pure water as any country in the world! Can you drink it? You cannot. They have a huge airport. Not one drinking fountain. Huge train depot in Oslo! Same thing. Big bus station! No fountains. So, with all this water in the country, how can you get a drink of water? You buy it. They sell these small bottles of water for two or three bucks apiece, bottles that are made out of the kind of plastic that is perhaps the number one pollution source in the world. Sure, they make an effort to recycle, but still. And they think they are so environmentally conscious! Gimme a break!

"Well, anyhow, Ellie was going to go fill that bottle with water from the rest room sink. I mean, it was not quite like getting it from the toilet bowl, but it was still a bit disgusting. But we were damned if we were going to pay three bucks for something that should be free! Well, Ellie came back with the bottle filled with water—not cold, of course—and we start off north. We've gone about ten miles or so, and all of a sudden she screams so loud that I nearly drive off the road. 'I left my purse in that toilet in the gas station,' she cries. 'We've got to go back for it!'

"Well of course we would go back for it, and I tell her that the next exit is only about three or four miles up the road. 'It might not be there by then,' she wails. 'It has all that money that we just withdrew from the ATM machine, it's got my driver's license and all the pictures of the kids. It has the directions to get to your relatives. Oh no! It even has my passport! Look, there's one of those emergency turn-around places for ambulances and squad cars. Take that and we'll go back right away.'

"'We can't take that,' I told her. 'I'm sure that would be against the law in Norway, just as it is in America. That's for emergencies,' I point out.'

"'What do you think this is?' she says. 'Take it right now!'"

"So, this is what I did, and pay attention now because this is important. I carefully signal and change lanes, then I carefully signal and get on the shoulder of the road and reach the turn-around place without incident. I carefully wait for a let up in the traffic so that I can get in. There is none. I pull onto the shoulder and slowly advance, signaling my intention all the time. Not one driver let me in! Not one. Had I been driving one of those big Mercedes that they seem to favor, I could have done it, but the only thing I could afford to rent was this little Fiat. I have never witnessed anything so discourteous on American highways. Finally, I just rather forced my little car in and did the best I could to speed up. You should have heard the noise. Every one of those rude bastards laid on their horn and many made some kind of gesture at me. I'm not sure what that was supposed to mean, but it didn't mean 'Welcome to Norway,' I can tell you that. Well, I carefully signaled and made my way into the slow lane.

"So I get back to that gas station, and I turn off on the exit, and all of a sudden there is this squad car with more lights on a vehicle than I have ever seen. He turns on his siren which may have been heard at least as far away as Scotland. I explain the situation and he follows me up to the station. Ellie gets out and one of the cops follows her to the restroom—not inside, but almost. Well, the good news was her purse was still there. Okay, so time for a concerned word to the tourist about Norwegian driving regulations and a wishing of welcome for your stay in Norway, right?

"Instead, I get a fifteen-minute lecture filled with recriminations and reminders every few words about putting lives in danger. I felt like belting the snot-nosed kid in his sparkling pressed uniform. Let me put it this way, he was as resplendent in his uniform as you are in yours. It kind of reminded me of a German S.S. soldier. Of course, the guy is holding my license in his hand the whole time, so I know enough to keep my mouth shut except for profuse apologies. I asked what was going on, and he says something to the effect that the usual procedure in this case would be to confiscate the car and arrest me, but they were trying to locate a judge. It must have been during that time that you were contacted. Anyway, they confer and tell me that the judge has agreed to let us go, but that I will not be permitted to drive in Norway ever again—not much chance of that!—and that Ellie will have to do the driving. Fortunately, as I have just pointed out, she now had her license because the purse was still there. As we prepared to go, and after he had handed my license back to me, one of those cops said that I was lucky that the judge 'liked Americans,' implying he did not. But, here's the kicker on this. It turns out that there were no surveillance cameras to record what I had done. The police had not seen the incident. So how did they know? Well, every one of those Mercedes and BMWs drivers had whipped out their cell phones and ratted me out! Those holier-than-thou prigs, this nation of tattle-tales, all took time to pull the stick out of their asses and fink on me. How did they know I wasn't taking my wife to the hospital? How did they know I wasn't delivering some life-saving serum? They didn't! They were just too busy minding somebody else's business!"

Orly could see, by the smoke that was coming out of Palmer's ears, that this was an event that would not soon be forgotten. He calmly said, "So, the old country wasn't quite what you expected?"

Palmer rather sheepishly calmed down. "It was fine. Lovely, in fact. I just got carried away because I thought it would be something I could certainly keep a secret from anybody in Minnesota—especially you. I mean, how would that play in the newspapers? 'MINNESOTA SHERIFF BANNED FROM DRIVING IN NORWAY FOR LIFE!' I probably would not win the next election—if I decide to run, that is. No, really. Nice people, and that area of North Hedeland is spectacular. That isn't the fjord area, of course, but it has one the magnificent Tron, which means 'throne,' one of the highest mountains in Norway, and it has the longest river, the Glomma, and it has cows, and picturesque villages. You should see Vingelen. I think that is sort of protected by the government. I saw the place where my grandfather was born. It was a huge house that was built in two sections, the *gammal hus*, or old house, dating from the 1600s, and the *ny hus*, or new house, dating from the 1700s. The outbuildings have sod for roofs, and since it is always raining up there, the roofs are always thick with green grass. Norway, of course, has money up the wazoo, so everything is tidy, there are little museums all over, and this Tynset town, where we stayed, has this wonderful new theatre. I don't know who designed it, but he was indeed a clever fellow."

"Have any lutefisk?"

"No, and I didn't ask for it. I had some lefse, though. We have better lefse here. Carl's Lefse, made in Hawley, is still the best in the world. And I ate a lot of cheese, usually Jarlsberg, but they pretty much eat the same things we do. They put down a lot of pizza, and I suppose they eat their share of meat, although I don't see how they can afford it. It is amazing just to walk through their grocery stores. Uffda! We were staying with these cousins in Tynset, and they were going to make their Norwegian version of pizza, so I thought I would buy a little beer to go with it. They sell 3.2 beer in the grocery store, so I checked it out. It cost almost ten bucks a can! Ten bucks! You can almost buy a case of the cheap stuff for that price here—my preferred brand. But by and large, everybody has cable television, everybody carries a cell phone, they all speak English—some better than others, of course—and naturally they all look like half the population of Fergus Falls."

Orly, the Swede, couldn't help himself. "But you liked Sweden, you say."

"Yah, we did. I think Stockholm is one of the most beautiful, efficient, and interesting cities I have ever experienced. They have this old ship that is one of the most amazing things I have ever seen. Back in 1628, when the Thirty Years War was going on, the king, Gustavus Adolphus, who really wanted a college in St. Peter named after him, ordered this huge battleship to be built. It was probably the largest ship ever built up to that time. The mast was a hundred and seventy feet tall. Anyway, since it was a battleship, they thought they should have a lot of cannons on it. When it was launched, it sailed off for about a hundred yards and then sank, taking all of those cannons and a lot of sailors down with it. Well, it sat at the bottom of the harbor for the next three hundred and thirty years, until a guy found it and then they fished it out of the drink, dried it off, treated it with preservatives, and there it is in this swell Vasa museum. Seeing that thing was worth the whole trip to Sweden.

"Stockholm is called the Venice of the North because much of it is built on islands, and that's where the old town, with old palaces and churches, is located. Of course, we wanted to spend some time in the modern city, mainly because Ellie wanted to go into the NK store. That's sort of like Stockholm's Harrods. While she was doing that, I went for a walk and found this central park area and they had a big beer tent set up, and you know what was in it?"

"Um … let me see … beer?"

"Well, yah, that, too, but there was an Elvis impersonator doing Elvis songs. Ah, the Scandinavian culture! And we drove through a lot of the smaller towns, which are clean and neat, naturally, and there is something about not being hemmed in by mountains. I suppose I liked it so much because it was just like Minnesota. You don't have to be ashamed about being a Swede."

"I never have."

"As you have always made abundantly clear! So what's happened since I've been gone? Any great crime wave?"

"Not particularly, but we need coffee if we are going to talk shop, don't we? I have a report all prepared, and I'll duck into my office for that and then get us a couple of cuppas."

The sheriff sat down and grinned ruefully. He was going to have to tone down the outrage for the Norwegian cops and refrain from bringing it up again. But still ...

Orly returned with the coffee, sat down, and opened his report. Palmer automatically reached for his coffee and took a sip. *My God, this is awful*, he thought. Aloud he said, "You know, Orly, they really know how to make coffee over there in Europe. I suppose we could start buying that more expensive stuff for the office, like that Swedish Gevalia, but I doubt if anybody around here could make it like that. So, whatcha got?"

Orly glanced at his report and replied, "Shortly after you left, there was a big spike in DWIs, but that coincided with what we have every year at this time. They have that big country music festival in Detroit Lakes—WeFest—and sure as

God made little green apples, a number of the people who come for it manage to find a resort in Otter Tail County. So, first of all, more drunks. Therefore, we double the number of patrol cars in that area. More drunks, more cops, more arrests, more revenue for us. And this year was really no different. There have been a few break-ins, the water patrol has been pretty busy, the town cops write parking tickets, and the highway patrol catches speeders, but there has been nothing extraordinary."

"No violence?"

"Not really. A bunch of college kids rented a cabin and invited about fifty other kids and that got noisy and a fight broke out. I sent a couple of deputies over and thy handled it. Oh, and I went out on a domestic myself. Do you know 'Wild Bill' Bjerke?"

"That rat-faced drunk? I suppose I don't know him, but he has been a guest of the county a couple of times. Why, what happened?"

"We got a 911 call from his wife. She thought he was going to kill her. I went out there. You know, I'm always a little scared about those domestics. You never know what's going to happen. But it was such a quiet night that I had sent most of the deputies home, and I just thought I should handle it myself. Call me paranoid, but I went out armed."

"Probably not a bad idea! As you say, those things are totally unpredictable. What was it all about, anyway?"

"It seems that Betty Bjerke had actually stopped in at Mabel Murphy's for a drink with another man—some scruffy looking guy with long hair, according to what Wild Bill told me—and he had gotten this helpful bit of information from a couple of his drinking buddies."

"And I presume Wild Bill did not like that."

"No, he did not. And he had put down quite a few of those twelve ounce curls."

"Was he drunk?"

"Let me put it his way. He was snockered, he was blithered, he was stewed to the gills, he was three sheets to the wind, he was blind drunk, he was feeling no pain, drunk as a skunk, and pissed as a newt. Furthermore, he was one of the most ornery cusses I have ever had to deal with. Still, I don't think he was really dangerous. Mrs. Bjerke, however, was sporting quite the shiner, and she claimed that he was going for his shotgun and planned to use it on her and her new boyfriend. Anyhow, I got him calmed down, and his wife was able to convince him that she had never done anything to be ashamed of and had never done that kind of thing before and that she had been neglected, and then she cried and cried and protested over and over again that nothing had happened with the guy at the bar. Which, apparently, it had not."

"Did you get the name of the would-be boyfriend?"

Peterson looked away and with a tinge of embarrassment said, "I didn't ask. I suppose I should have, but, well, you had to have been there. Apparently Wild Bill beat it out of Betty, however, but I never heard a name."

"So, what did you do?"

Orly gave a large shrug and replied, "Wild Bill had really started to sober up, and he seemed oh so remorseful, and I just told him he should comfort and forgive his wife and had better hope that she would forgive him for giving her a black eye. I had just been reading a British 'Whodunit,' and so I told him to make her a cup of tea. I made all sorts of threats, warning him not to go around blabbing about a shotgun and about what would happen next time, and then I left."

"Think it'll help?"

"It might. I ran into Betty at the grocery store a couple of days ago, and she told me that Wild Bill had promised to stop drinking and that he apparently is keeping his word."

"Well then, good job. Anything else?"

"Well, there was this incident out at the Otter Tail County Fair, not long ago. There was this so-called artist who got punched in the face and called us up and wanted to press charges. It seems he does caricatures and did one of some guy's daughter and that, well, let's just say there was a dispute as to the merits of the portrait."

"So, did you arrest the guy?"

"No, because nobody knew who he was. This artist, some guy with a Finnish name, didn't know who it was, and nobody around admitted to seeing the so-called assault. We told him that we would 'keep the file open'—whatever that is supposed to mean—on the case. Well, unless some guy comes in here bragging about punching some long-haired artist on the nose, I don't think we will hear any more about it."

"You know, I think I know who that artist is. He's one of these long-haired bearded artists who has a little tent every year at the Phelps Mill celebration. He sells cheap jewelry and those painted boards as well. He seems to sell a lot of that stuff. I think his name is Kivi or something."

"Say, you don't suppose that is the guy that Betty Bjerke …"

CHAPTER SEVEN

"Sex appeal is the keynote of our civilization."

– Henri Bergson

The sheriff settled back in his office and attempted to catch up on his neglected paperwork. It was depressing to see how much awaited him. There were budget requests, meeting notices, new policies to be implemented or considered, and reports from the county commission meetings with items concerning the sheriff's office highlighted. There was an invitation to speak at a regional conference sponsored by the North Dakota State University Criminal Justice Department. There were also a couple of hundred e-mails. He scanned the e-mails first, deleting those that had no importance whatsoever, answering a few that seemed urgent, and deciding to save the rest for another time. He arranged the paperwork into urgent, important, and less important, and threw the rest into the wastebasket. By this time, it was three o'clock, and he became aware of the effects of jet lag. It was, after all, ten p.m. in Oslo.

He drove home and put his pride-and-joy Acura into the garage and called out to his other pride and joy, Ellie, "I'm home." He found her asleep on the couch, covered with three weeks of mail and the telephone in her hand. He quietly gazed upon her and was once again overwhelmed by how much he loved her. She looked so peaceful in the arms of Morpheus, her dark blond hair with several streaks of grey spread across the back of the sofa but one strand adhered to the corner of her mouth. Palmer thought back through the forty years that they had been married, and back to when she had been a campus radical in slashed blue jeans. Over the years he had often gazed at her while she slept, and there was no more beautiful sight in the word than to see her open her beautiful green eyes. They were empty nesters now. Maj, Amy, and Trygve had all graduated from Gustavus Adolphus, Concordia, and St. Olaf, and had turned into valued members of their new communities and were a perpetual source of pride. They were grandparents now, as Maj and her husband Jon had given to the world little Bjorn.

Palmer quietly went into the kitchen and heated two cups of coffee in the microwave. He went to the secret place in a kitchen drawer, the place where they had always hid the good chocolate from the kids, and found a treasure from their trip, a Freia Melkesjokolade bar, which had been purchased with the last of the kroner at the Oslo airport. He brought the cups and the chocolate into the living room, placed them on the coffee table, and once again took pleasure in seeing those green eyes open.

"Oh, Palmer," Ellie said with a yawn. "I must have fallen asleep. Oh, what a sweetheart! Norwegian chocolate and coffee! Just what I need!"

"Been talking on the phone?"

"Yes, I've talked to all three of the kids. They all send you greetings."

Palmer frowned and said, "I thought we were going to call them together."

"Well, I didn't call them, they called me. They didn't think that you would actually go to work the day after you got home. They all wanted to hear about our trip. By the time Amy called, I had gone through it twice and I began to think I was doing an imitation of Rick Steves."

Palmer grinned and said, "You know, I thought about each of them while we were on our trip, remembering many of the other trips that we took when they were little—the national parks, Winnipeg, Washington D.C. They were good kids then, and they are great kids now. Remember that saying that goes 'When children are born to parents that truly love each other, they will carry that love in their hearts for the rest of their lives'? Well, I don't know how wise we were as parents, but no one could deny that we gave them that. Did they have any news?"

"Oh, not too much, I suppose. They just told about what they were doing in their jobs, and the weather, of course. Trygve said he had sent some anti-Republican jokes in e-mail, but I haven't even had a chance to look at that yet. Oh, and Maj says that little Bjorn took his first steps yesterday."

Palmer shook his head and said, "That hardly seems possible, but if he is going to quarterback the Vikings someday, he has to start sooner or later. Um ... you didn't mention anything about that, you know, that episode with the Norwegian police, did you?"

Ellie had just taken a sip of coffee and almost spewed it out. "Why, wasn't I supposed to?"

"It's just something that I prefer did not get around, if you know what I mean. You gotta admit, it is not what people want to hear about their sheriff."

"Oh, I don't know …"

"I mean, it is not something that the sheriff would want them to hear about, all right? So, did you tell them?"

"Well … sort of."

"Sort of? Let's have it then."

"I didn't volunteer it, and I tried to avoid it because you weren't on the phone to defend yourself, but I was telling Maj how we were able to drive all over Norway and Sweden without any trouble and then she asked me if I ever drove over there and then I admitted that I had driven quite a bit actually and then she asked how come and I couldn't come up with a quick fib and, after all, you never said I couldn't tell anyone. But they don't see people from Fergus Falls much anymore so I don't think anybody else will hear of it."

"By this time she will have told Jon, and the next time she talks to either of her siblings it will be certain to be a topic of amusement. Which means every Christmas or Thanksgiving or any other family gathering it will be mentioned. By the time little Bjorn starts to talk, the first thing he will say is 'Grandpa isn't allowed to drive in Norway.' Before long, my brother Rolf will be preaching a sermon on it in church."

"I'm sorry. I didn't know it was a state secret. As the sergeant says in *Stripes*, 'Lighten up, Francis!' Besides, you gotta admit it was kind of funny!"

"Funny?"

"Yeah, it was hilarious. First of all, once they took your license I assumed they would do what an American cop would do, that is, run it through the database to see if you had any outstanding warrants. They would discover you were a peace officer and would extend you the same kind of professional courtesy that a shark in the water would extend to a lawyer. But anyway, so here you are, a paragon of virtue who has never jaywalked or kept a library book overdue for a day, being bawled out by some young cops. You should have seen your face. There was this kind of desperate, hurt look that seemed to beg forgiveness. And then when they spoke to you, you responded in this this spanked-boy tone that could only be said as fawning."

"Well, I would hardly call it fawning!"

"Are you kidding? Bambi never fawned that much! And as they went on and started talking about the judge and what they usually do in those circumstances, and I saw the look on your face, I started to think about you going to jail, the 'yale hus,' I suppose we could call it. And then I pictured smuggling in a file wrapped in a roll of lefse, and you busting out, and the two of us being chased by baying Norwegian elk hounds, and barely making the border of Sweden with its twenty-foot-high electrified barbed-wire fence with guard towers and searchlights, and then we would hijack somebody's Volvo and crash through the barrier. And finally, the docile, hangdog look as you climbed into the passenger seat and handed me the keys. Oh yes! From that will come a great family story, especially the way I will tell it."

"Since one is hardly aware of when one actually crosses the border from Norway into Sweden, you might tone it down a bit."

"Tone it down! By the time the kids come home for Christmas, I will have worked guns and explosives into the story."

"Oh, well, I suppose it doesn't make any difference. It's just that while we were sitting in that little Fiat and the cops were on the telephone, they used the time to call one Orly Peterson to check on my *bona fides*. God only knows how many people he has told. So who cares? Anything in the mail?"

"We got a ton of travel literature from Grand Circle, Viking, and Vantage. Alumni magazines from four colleges. I suppose they think that in paying all that tuition, we would still be in the habit of sending them money. Still, it's kind of fun to look through them to see if any of our kids have wildly successful classmates. We got a few bills, nothing unexpected, and since the bank pays them automatically, there is nothing for us to do about them. I do rather fear next month's credit card bill, however. You know, it's amazing how little mail there actually is these days. We used to get a weekly thing from the church, but now even that is online.

"There is one thing that could be interesting, however. We got this thing from the Lake Region Arts Council. There's going to be an opening of a new show at the River Inn building next week. I think I'd kinda like to go."

"Oh yah? Who's the artist?"

"It's some guy named Alek Kivi. You ever heard of him?"

"Funny you should mention that. Orly and I were just talking about him. He said that some dissatisfied father took one look at the picture he had done of his daughter and went over and slugged him. Kivi wanted to charge him with assault, but since the man immediately left after putting Kivi right on his hind end, he never got his name. Orly could only tell him that it would be hard to arrest anyone without knowing who to charge, and he got a little put out with the sheriff's office. And then, get this, he might have been the cause of a domestic disturbance. It seems a longhaired artist type met another man's wife for a glass of wine at Mabel Murphy's. The guy found out, beat up his wife, and wanted to take a shotgun to find her 'lover.' Fortunately, when Orly got there, he was able to calm him down and put the fear of God into him about toting a shotgun around. But can you beat that! I mean, how many local longhaired artists do we have around here? I actually met Kivi last summer at that Phelps Mill wing-ding. In fact, you were there, too. He was that scruffy-looking guy who did awful caricatures of people, sold crappy jewelry, and peddled some sort of barn-shadow things. Do you remember him? He looked like he spent his time sleeping under the bridge, chugging wine. His clothes were appalling and he smelled. I remember him as a sneaky, wimpy sort of guy who no woman would ever look at twice. I find it very hard to believe that he is in some sort of love triangle."

"Oh, I don't know. I can see it."

Palmer jerked his head back and blinked twice. "What? You can't be serious. What could any woman find attractive in him?"

"Well," Ellie began cautiously, "when we talked to him, he had a way of looking deeply into my eyes, like he was really listening to me. I mean he had those deep-set dark eyes that seemed to imply that whatever I was saying was the most interesting thing in the world."

"His eyes! They had all the animation of a dead bass! Maybe he was just drunk and couldn't focus. His eyes! Gimme a break!"

"And you know, Palmer, you might think of him as scruffy, but that stubble-beard thing is kind of the 'in thing' now. Just look at Brad Pitt sometimes. And that artist is still rather young. And slim. I can see where an older woman might be flattered by his attentions."

Palmer shook his head in disgust while unconsciously sucking in his gut. "Are you putting me on?"

"Listen, I happen to prefer my men with a bit of distinguished grey on their heads. I prefer light blue to 'dead bass,' and I prefer my men to be, er, somewhat less thin. I'm not saying I could ever go for someone like that, but that doesn't mean that some women wouldn't go for him."

Palmer stared, and in spite of the fact that he considered himself a dedicated feminist, could only mutter, "Women!"

"What did you say, dear?"

"Um, I was just thinking maybe we should go to that opening. I think I need to take another look at that Finn."

CHAPTER EIGHT

"True friends stab you in the front."

– Oscar Wilde

It was workshop time at Fergus Falls State University. Before the start of every academic year, all departments would meet to discuss policies and budget requests for the next two semesters. For some reason, and in spite of a great deal of determination from every artist, not a single member of the art department had come up with a valid reason to skip the whole thing, and for the first time in years they were all there. The seminar room was clean and tidy, a condition that would not be replicated until the following autumn. Wallace Duncan peered morosely at his staff. He recalled younger days when returning faculty would return to campus in at least semi-formal attire. Now everyone wore shorts, sandals, and T-shirts. Not that he could complain, since he had led the retreat from sartorial splendor and now wore hiking shorts, a red LACMA T-shirt, and was barefoot. He peeked surreptitiously at his watch. The department meeting could just not go on much longer. One hour that he would never get back in life! Duncan was chair of the Department of Art at Fergus Falls State University and was listening to the tedious painting teacher, Sherwin Williams, make his annual plea for more prominent spaces around the campus for excellent faculty art. *If I saw excellent faculty art, I might be able to find a place for it*, Duncan thought, but finally pacified his faculty member with the usual fib. "I've been looking into it, Sherwin, and the vice president and I are kicking around a few good ideas." They had already ruminated upon the budget, student retention, the scheduling of the student art show, and next year's faculty art show; bellyached about the high cost of textbooks, paint, clay, and welding supplies; deplored the scheduled calendar changes; and made snide comments about the music faculty, with whom they shared the Joan Mondale Center for the Arts.

"So ... if there's nothing else ...?"

"Well, there is just one more thing I think we should discus," Williams, a thin man of early middle years and sporting MOMA T-shirt, stated pugnaciously.

Oh, God! Let this be over! thought Duncan, but aloud he said, "What is it, Sherwin?"

Williams puffed out his cheeks, huffed, and said, "I don't know if the rest of you have heard this, but do you know who the Lake Region Arts Council has chosen to have a show at the River Inn Gallery next week?"

This would not be news to everyone, but a few raised eyebrows and scowls were unanimously turned to the painter, and suspicious eyes darted around the room. Wallace Duncan was the art historian, and although he dabbled in photography and was quite competent at that craft, he had no intention of publicly showing his work. Clay Morton, the ceramicist, however, had been working on a series of pots that, as a group, represented, in abstract form, the seven deadly sins. Duncan knew that Morton had submitted a proposal to the Arts Council. Duncan also suspected that Williams had submitted a proposal, since he did so every year and was convinced it was only a matter of wearing down the council before his *trompe l'œil* paintings received the attention they deserved. Denise Steele, the sculptor, had been unusually productive, he thought, and who knew what the reclusive Maryann Stamp had been doing with her printmaking?

"All right, Goddammit, who?" said Morton, wearing a shapeless clay-encrusted shirt that complimented his clay-encrusted bald head. He was always unappreciative of Williams' theatricality. "I just returned home from Spain last night. I thought all of that had been settled."

Williams looked at each member of his department in turn, savoring the moment, and finally blurted out "Alek Kivi."

"Oh for God's sake, who told you that?" Ms. Steele, a tall, muscular woman with a face set in a permanent challenge, retorted.

"It's true. I was just at the art council offices this morning. I saw the poster. It opens tomorrow night!"

"What were you doing there?" Duncan asked. "I thought you had soured on them ever since they rejected your last proposal."

"Well, I had submitted a new proposal, and I had reason to believe that I was a leading candidate for the next show," replied Williams, defensively. An unidentified snort followed that statement. "I just stopped down there for a few minutes to see when they would be considering the upcoming schedule. When they told me it was going to be Kivi, I thought they were joking. I'm afraid I made a rather rude and unprofessional comment and, quite frankly, they resented it. But it is true."

The soft-voiced Mrs. Stamp did not use her soft voice to exclaim: "Bullshit!" Her voice was not often heard, even when she thought she was shouting, for everyone seemed to overlook the diminutive brunette with the Monet print top.

Morton said, "You took the word right out of my mouth, Maryann, but what are we going to do about it?"

There were several spontaneous comments, but Ms. Steele shouted, "I'll tell you what I am going to do. I am going to go down there and demand an explanation. All of us have *vitae* that record our accomplishments in our respective fields. All of us can provide some kind of testimony from our fellow artists. I daresay that we have all written recommendations for each other. I think I can also presume that none of us has ever provided anything along those lines for Kivi. So here we are—the academic citadel of Fergus Falls—and they give a show to a faker, a mountebank, a charlatan, a fraud like Kivi?" Williams did not know what a mountebank was, but he figured it was nothing good, and cheered her on. "This cannot stand!" Ms. Steele continued. "What do you think, Bonnie?"

The men of the department did not particularly care what kind of T-shirt Bonnie Lassie was wearing, since she filled out each one spectacularly. The part-time painting instructor, who had astounded the art world with her abstract paintings the previous summer, calmly said, "I suppose it would be immodest of me to protest that I had never considered myself to be in the same artistic circle of Alek Kivi, but all in all, I have to agree with Maryann."

"The problem is he's lazy. The problem is he drinks. The problem is he's crazy. The problem is he stinks," wryly contributed Duncan, selecting appropriate words from *West Side Story*. "Yeah, yeah, yeah, we all agree as to the artistic and personal merit of Kivi. But Lake Region was put in very bad situation. Their big show with that Danish artist was cancelled only last month. Harriet Monroe, in her role as executive director, tried to contact us, but apparently we were all out of town at the time. The whole Kivi thing came out of a somewhat frantic and contentious meeting last month, and, just among us, Harriet feels as bad about it as you do. I don't want any of you to go over there and start a diatribe against the arts council. Apparently Williams has already put Harriet's knickers in a twist—she called me just after he stormed out this morning—and we don't need any more of that. We have always had the best in the way of relationships and co-operation, and for our mutual success in the future, this attitude must continue. I will make a formal appointment with the Harriet and try to get to the bottom of this. Meanwhile, moan among yourselves all you want, but don't talk about it in the halls, don't mention it to your students—that means you, Sherwin—and don't even talk about it to other members of other departments. If I hear about it from anybody else on campus, I will assume it came from one of you.

"As preposterous as it may seem, I can kind of see how this could have happened. In Otter Tail County, and in all of the counties that surround us, whose art is most commonly hanging in the homes? It's not Sherwin's clever paintings, it's not Clay's pots, nor is it ten foot piece of metal by Denise. Nope, there are caricatures of family members, boards with a horse or a tractor silhouette, or some sappy greeting card. I think "folk art" would be too nice a word for Kivi's rubbish, and to call it 'primitive art' would be to insult a cave man. But let's face it—a lot of people went for that Grandma Moses stuff, and it really is quite awful. I would be willing to bet that those poor people at Lake Region, bless their hearts, have been under tremendous pressure to feature an 'artist of the people.' It's enough to gag a maggot, but, well, I'm not going to judge them if they only did what they had to do. I think that it is at a time like this that Lake Region needs us more than ever. The reception for the opening of Kivi's show is tomorrow night. I would like you all to be there. To be sure, I can't make you, but, let's face it, it could even be sort of fun. For now, just go home," Duncan ended, picturing a very large martini under a very shady tree.

CHAPTER NINE

"Art is making something out of nothing and selling it."

– Frank Zappa

The opening for *Magic in Minimalism: The Art of Alek Kivi* was held at the River Inn Gallery at seven-thirty on a warm night in the middle of August. Ms. Monroe and the staff of the Lake Region Arts Council had been bravely determined not to lower their standards for an arts opening. The art, such as it was, was professionally displayed and gladioli of various and interesting colors adorned the first two rooms. Most guests entered from the door opening to the street, and found themselves in a room bathed in sunlight, a marvelous room that had once been the hotel coffee shop. The first room held Kivi's collection of caricatures, while the second room displayed numerous farm silhouettes, a table covered with jewelry and greeting cards, and a buffet table featuring *hors d'oeuvres* and a punch bowl.

As an extra, added feature of the opening, the artist had insisted on including an "artist at work" display in the third room. This third room had been the exquisite dining hall of the hotel, and had recently held the meeting that had given rise to Kivi's invitation. In addition to a place for the board to meet, however, the room also served as the office of the executive director. A large, seven-foot-high screen had been erected to isolate Ms. Monroe's work area, and this provided extra space on which to pin the artist's sketches. Kivi had set up an easel with an eighteen- by twenty-four-inch canvas, a stool, and a table on which a small glass palette was precariously perched. Tonight the subject was a still life, featuring pears, apples, bananas, and, somewhat incongruously, a teddy bear. The medium was acrylic and, perhaps fortunately, the artist had not gotten very far. He had two brushes, both smeared with paint, and a very new rag. Whenever anyone came into his "artist working" space, he was only too glad to hold his brush in an imperial manner and deign to speak to his guests, thus, again perhaps fortunately, delaying the further progress of the painting.

To everyone's surprise, the rooms were full of "art" patrons, and it was generally conceded that it was the largest crowd ever to attend an art opening. Palmer and Ellie Knutson were there, although each was more interested in the artist than the art. This would be understandable in any case. Early on, Palmer had wandered in to watch the "artist" "working." After a very short time, he came back and whispered in Ellie's ear, "You were just putting me on, right? I mean, no way could that man attract a woman with normal eyesight." Ellie just shrugged and said enigmatically, "That just shows what you know about things."

Palmer drifted away and examined a few of the caricatures. A voice beside him said, "Vell, *har du setti.* Are yew in town tew?" The fake Norwegian accent was terrible, of course, but Palmer smiled to see his deputy standing there with a glass of punch in his hand.

"Jah, I'm in town tew. Vat are yew doing here den? So now you're a patron of the arts?"

Orly gestured to his very pregnant wife and said, "In fact, Allysha and I come to most of these openings. She enjoys coming here and meeting artists and trying to give me just a patina of culture. She didn't know anything about this Kivi or his art, but as she put it, this might be the last time we can go out together for a very long time, and when we do we will have to hire a babysitter. I can't believe this crowd! By the way, did you go into the other room and watch the artist "at work"?

"Yah I did. That guy can't possibly be the guy that Betty Bjerke had a drink with, could it?"

"Are you kidding? If there's one man we can cross off our list, it would be him. Can you believe any woman would willingly want to be seen with him? I mean, if that were to be true, where does that put the rest of us guys, huh?"

"Exactly!" Palmer said, nodding enthusiastically. "Still, when I mentioned the possibility that he had tried to hit on another man's wife to Ellie, in a joking 'Have you ever heard of anything more preposterous?' way, she said she could see it. Case in point, see that nice looking woman over there standing next to those flowers?"

"Yeah, what about her? Who is she?"

"Ellie told me that she is the artist's wife."

After a silence, Orly merely said, "Huh. Go figure!" They surveyed the room for a few minutes until suddenly Orly blurted out, "Oh my God, look who's here!"

Palmer followed Orly's gaze until he saw ... "Don't tell me. Is that really Wild Bill Bjerke? He is wearing a coat and tie. He is shaved. He has a neat haircut. And, most implausibly, he seems sober. Is that Mrs. Bjerke hanging on his arm?"

"None but. I couldn't be more surprised than if I had seen a blind man checking out the drawings."

"In this case," Palmer muttered, "he would be the lucky one."

The crowd continued to grow. The artist was scheduled to present a gallery talk at eight-thirty, and the *hors d'oeuvres* were disappearing at an alarming rate. Palmer mingled and chatted and kept his ears open. In the unlikely event that he would be asked for his opinion of the show, he wanted to sound reasonably informed.

"'Magic in Minimalism'! Gimme a break! Do you think he has the slightest idea what minimalism is?" "Of course not. Perhaps he is just into alliteration." (Mean-spirited giggles.) "Perhaps it refers to how one can get a gallery show with a minimum of talent." "Who do you suppose he had to blackmail to get a show of his own?" "Who or how many? (A short guffaw.)

"Did you see that jewelry in the other room? Amazing what one can do with a few beads, some wire, some feathers, and a leather shoe lace, huh?" "Yeah, it makes one appreciate those 'What Would Jesus Do?' rubber bands. Hey Jill, how did you like the artist's jewelry?" "It made me long for a case of arthritis so I could wear one of those copper bracelets instead." (Other mean-spirited giggles.) "Not me, I'd prefer wearing a long-sleeved blouse, even in this weather. And how about those broaches?" "Is that what they are? I thought they were some kind of Junior Woodchuck badge." (A loud snorting guffaw.)

In one corner of the room there was a series of caricatures of political figures. Amazingly, several of them had a round gold sticker affixed to the bottom, indicating that they had been sold. A voice said, "Are you kidding me? Who would ever buy such things?" "Funny you should ask. I noticed who purchased the Hillary Clinton and Barak Obama sketches. It was the chair of the Otter Tail County Republican Party." (Sniggering.) "Of course, who else? I can see them in the window of party headquarters with a speech balloon with something nasty being said. How about the Reagan and Bush and Cheney ones? Who do you suppose bought them?" "I can't say, but I wouldn't doubt if they would reappear as a door prize at the next Jackson/Jefferson day celebration for the Democrats." (Deeper voiced mean-spirited laughter ensued.)

In the other room, near the punchbowl, Palmer heard, "And those silhouettes. It's a shame that someone would spoil a perfectly good piece of firewood by putting all those chemicals on it." Someone else shamelessly held up his fingers and made a shadow image of a bunny.

Another voice said, "Notice how about half of those silhouettes are shorter than the others? You can see where he sawed them off, did a little sanding, and spread more varnish. There used to be a picture of my house there. I came all the way down here just to make sure he wasn't still using my copyrighted design." "What would you have done if he were still using your design?" "Good question. I considered suing, but I doubt I would get much from him. A nice little scandal would fix his wagon, though. Look over at this one. It looks like a different house, but this is my house, too. He has just used a different angle for his photo, and it might be harder to prove that it was my house, but still ... I warned him."

"You know, they've really done a good job in rehabilitating this old hotel. The lobby is stately and clean. Everything is kept up. The old rooms are now apartments, with kitchens, new bathrooms, you name it." "Yup, it's really pretty nice. Have you seen that urinal in the men's room?" "You mean that odd triangle thing so you can carry on a face to face conversation with your buddy while you are taking a whiz? Priceless! I wonder if any other of them things exist anymore? Have you ever seen any of the rooms?" "Oh yeah. After my dad died, my wife and I and our family moved into my folks' place, and my mother moved into one of these apartments. She may have been the very first resident. It is just the place for her. I mean, it's warm, safe, and close to the Viking Café, her hairdresser, and her church. Just a block off of Lincoln Avenue, so she can walk around and shop, nipping into Lundeen's to fondle their gift selection. She's getting pretty long in the tooth now, of course, but it's really close to the hospital. Oh, yeah, it's perfect." "I was just thinking, you know, that everything is still intact. I mean, the front desk of the hotel is still in place. If somebody wanted to open one to those boutique hotels, well, hell, it wouldn't take much to turn it back into a hotel again. And look at that swell dining room where that artist is."

At eight-fifteen, Harriet Monroe announced that the artist would only be working for five more minutes and would then close his activity to take a few minutes in private to prepare for his gallery talk. A few of the people who had not visited the "artist working" area walked in and made a quick loop around the artist who was now intensely staring at his canvas and his fruit and his teddy bear. Shortly afterwards, the executive director had succeeded in herding all of the curious or amused patrons out of the old dining room. The door was firmly closed behind her.

"So, are you staying for the talk?" "I wouldn't miss it for the world. I want to find out just how he makes those lovely farm shadows. We have one of them in our home, you know?" "So, are you staying for the talk?" "Are you kidding? I wouldn't miss it for the world. I mean, how can anyone explain, let alone defend, this dreck?"

"Hey, any of that there punch left?"

At the precise time of eight-thirty, nothing happened. Nothing happened for the next ten minutes. At a quarter to nine, the assembled collection of fans and critics began to get nervous. Harriet Monroe knocked on the door and asked, "Are you just about ready, Mr. Kivi? ... Mr.Kivi? ... Mr. Kivi, will you please unlock this door?" There was nothing but silence.

An LRAC board member appeared at her elbow and whispered, "I think you should open the door. You must have a key!"

"Of course I have a key! It's my office. So where do I keep my keys? In my purse, which I keep, naturally, in my office! Is anybody about to volunteer to break the door down?"

Bertram Flom stepped forward and said, "There's no need for that. Swen Walstrom, the custodian, has a little office in the basement. He's always around when we have an event. Somebody go down and get Swen."

"Why don't you go yourself," Ms. Adams replied, "since you seem to know where to find him?"

"Er, well, all right."

A short time later Swen stood next to Harriet and unlocked the door. Harriet barged in and suddenly let out an odd gasp, followed by a rather forlorn moan. Swen put his arm around her, pulled her back, and said. "Stay back, stay back. Is there a doctor in the house?"

Palmer Knutson gave his head a slight shake. He thought, *Did he really just say 'Is there a doctor in the house?'* When no doctor spoke up, all eyes began to turn to the sheriff. Palmer pushed his way to the door and Swen whispered in his ear. Palmer nodded. He announced, "There seems to have been some sort of accident. Please do not try to come in. Is Orly Peterson still here?"

"Yeah, right here, Palmer. What can I do?"

"Just come in with me. And, ladies and gentlemen, I will come out and give you some information as to what has happened shortly. Meanwhile, please do not leave the building."

Orly and Palmer entered the room and quickly closed the door behind them. Alek Kivi lay on the floor with unfocused eyes staring up at the ceiling. A trickle of blood ran from his right temple down to his ear and onto the floor. Two new Winsor and Newton Artist's Acrylic paintbrushes were crammed up his nostrils and into his brain.

"I think we can rule out suicide," Orly helpfully stated.

CHAPTER TEN

"Murder is unique in that it abolishes the party it injures, so that society has to take the place of the victim and on his behalf demand atonement or grant forgiveness; it is the one crime in which society has a direct interest."

– W. H. Auden

Palmer Knutson had been involved with murder cases before. He felt that familiar sense of an adrenalin flow and overwhelming duty to take charge.

"Right, then, Orly! I presume you have your telephone with you. You stay here and call for Doc Clark, a scene-of-the-crime squad, and forensics. Call the Fergus Falls Police Department and have them send over anyone they can spare—we have a crowd out there. Look around for any evidence that may be apparent, but don't touch anything!" Palmer noticed a short look of resentment from his deputy and said, "I'm sorry, Orly, I didn't need to say that. We'll want to make sure that no one leaves. Once we have arranged to have the exit secured, I'll want you to get the names, addresses, and phone numbers for everyone left in the building. Meanwhile, I'll have to find the widow and tell her what has happened."

Orly nodded, but asked, "What are you going to tell her? That someone murdered her husband by cramming two paintbrushes in his brain?

"No, give me some credit. I'm not going to tell her that. Besides, that isn't the truth."

"What?"

Knutson left the room and quickly closed the door behind him. He strode to the exit, blocking it with his body, and announced, "Ladies and gentlemen, I'm afraid that there has been a serious incident. In a short time my deputy will be out here to take all of your names and addresses before you will be allowed to leave. I must ask you to remain in the gallery until we have collected this information. I assure you that none of you is in any danger, but it may take some time to sort things out. Other personnel from the sheriff's office and the police department will be arriving soon. I ask for your patience and your cooperation." The sheriff looked toward the door, behind which the late artist was sprawled on the floor with paintbrushes in his brain, and saw the woman who was now a widow. "Mrs. Kivi? I must speak to you in private."

Palmer led a perplexed Mrs. Kivi to a corner of the room beyond the by-now-empty punchbowl. He knew from experience that there was never a way to sugarcoat this message. "I'm afraid that I have some terrible news for you," he said. "Your husband is dead. He appears to have been the victim of an attack. The scene is incredibly disturbing. What we have to do now would be extremely upsetting to you, so I suggest that you wait out here until we are ready to take your husband away. There will be a doctor and an investigative team and there will be a number of photographs that need to be taken. I wish to spare you this, and when we finish he will be as you will always want to remember him. Frankly, I'm not sure that I have the right to ask this of you, but there is nothing you can do for him, and I firmly believe that this would be the best thing for you at this time. Is there anyone special here that you can turn to? We will do everything we can to arrange for everything. Please trust me on this."

Mrs. Kivi heard most of what he said between sobs, nodded, and buried her face in Palmer's shirt. He noticed a woman about Mrs. Kivi's age who was hovering nearby and raised his eyebrows slightly and made a small movement with his hand. The woman rushed up and took Mrs. Kivi in her arms while telling Knutson, "I'm her sister."

The sheriff ducked his head into the dining room that had morphed into a murder room and called his deputy out to assist in crowd control. Already in the distance they could hear a siren announcing that help was on the way. Orly huddled with Palmer and whispered, "I found something rather strange on the floor next to the body. It appears to be several grains of sand. Do you think I should check for anyone who has sand on his shoes?"

"I noticed that, too. And I think it is important. And yet, people have been in and out of that room for the last hour, and could have left it there long before the murder. There are just too many people out there now. Still, keep your eyes open. If someone is trailing a lot of sand, detain them and find out why. Most of them are local, or, at least, are not from any great distance away. Take them two at a time. That way, if anybody was contemplating giving a false address, he would be less likely to do it with a witness. Get rid of them as soon as you can—guests, staff, all of them but the widow and her sister. I told her she could wait until such time as her husband was, er, just a little more presentable. Meanwhile, direct the doctor and the forensics team to enter the Lake Region Arts Council offices from the hotel lobby. Oh, and ask Ellie to take Allysha home. We're going to be busy for a while."

Within a short time, other deputies, police officers, and the scene-of-the-crime staff arrived. Old Doctor Jimmy Clark, the Otter Tail Medical Examiner, entered, looking as though he did not know where he was, and he probably didn't. Seeing the condition of the late Alek Kivi, he winced and suddenly seemed to recollect his duty. Palmer left them all to do their jobs, and then rounded up a few police officers and deputies for a special sweep of the grounds immediately beneath the dining room balconies.

There was nothing below the balconies, but several feet away there was a dumpster and two parked cars. Beyond the small parking area was a concrete wall that separated the hotel property from the overgrown bushes that led down to the river. There was room on the balconies for only about four men each, so Palmer split them up and spoke to them loud enough for all to hear. "All right, listen up. I don't know what to tell you to look for, so just pick up whatever you find that may have some significance. A dropped pen, a handkerchief, a rubber glove—who knows what you might find? Of course, use common sense. An old beer can or a semi-decayed cigarette butt is hardly likely to be of use, but a fresh butt or a new can just might. But look carefully, and look fast, because it will be dark soon. Tomorrow I expect that a Bureau of Criminal Apprehension team will be here to do a more precise search. I want a couple of you to go beyond the wall and search around down by the river. Look for fresh footprints. There won't be any on the asphalt, of course, but there may be some along the edge or even by the river. It looks like a thunderstorm is coming, so right now it is imperative to find whatever we can before it is washed out by a storm."

The professional forensic team worked with speed, but with painstaking precision. Photographs of the body and the crime scene were extensive and complete. When this was completed, the doctor removed the paintbrushes from the nose of Mr. Kivi, washed the blood from the side of his face, and directed that he be put on a gurney. With the body wheeled out to the lobby, Mrs. Kivi was at last allowed to view her late husband. Perhaps she was all cried out, but in any event, as she stood there in the arms of her sister, she said, "He looks so peaceful. More peaceful than he has ever looked before." She patted his forehead and he soon disappeared into the ambulance.

By eleven o'clock the forensic team had finished their work, and Palmer and Orly stood looking at the bloodstained floor that had once known a breathing Alek Kivi. Outside, the air was still and humid. A curtain of lightning flashes appeared in the west. Inside, however, there was something about the murder scene that made the atmosphere even colder than the temperature pumped out by the overworked air conditioner. After a long silence, Orly said, "I never got a chance to ask you, but what did you mean when you said you weren't going to lie by telling Mrs. Kivi that her husband was murdered by paintbrushes crammed into his brain?"

Palmer shrugged, "Well, certainly you noticed that there was only a small amount of blood from each of his nostrils. In other words, he was already dead when the brushes were implanted. Furthermore, he was bleeding from the side of his head, just above the hairline. In other words, someone conked him, killed him, and then, for reasons best known to himself, or herself, decided to make a bit of a dramatic scene."

"Ah," Orly replied. "It did occur to me that it would be difficult to get a victim to oblige the murderer by staying still while the pointed end of a wooden brush was pounded into his head. Well, that makes a lot more sense. But did anyone find anything here that could have been used as the proverbial 'blunt instrument?'"

"No, and as much as I watched the scene of the crime team, they were very thorough. One of them specifically said that there was no object in this room that could have been used as a murder weapon. But then, I didn't think they would find the murder weapon in this room."

The deputy scowled. "What do you mean? Then what was used?"

"Tell me," Palmer said, "did you get a look at the list of items that were found during that preliminary search in the rear of the building?"

"Yeah, there didn't seem to be much of interest. Almost everything they picked up must have been lying there for days. They even found somebody's sock."

Palmer nodded and quietly said, "Uh huh, I rather thought they might."

"Let me get this straight, you expected them to find somebody's stocking?"

"Yup."

"Why, for God's sake?"

"Look, I don't think there is much more we can do here," Palmer said. "The storm is going to hit any minute, and one of the guys told me that there were severe weather warnings out. Time to go home! Let's make sure the doors are all locked and meet in my office tomorrow. I promise I will tell you about the sock."

CHAPTER ELEVEN

"Facts are stubborn things, but statistics are more pliable."

– Mark Twain

With a cheery "Good morning, Palmer," Orly Peterson, with a cup of coffee in each hand, pushed the door open with his foot.

"Ah, good man," the sheriff said, "Have a seat. Quite a storm last night, wasn't it? It was really coming down in buckets for a while. Did you ever hear how much rain we got?"

"I heard we got a little over an inch, but up by Pelican Rapids they got close to two inches."

"Uffda, that isn't good for the farmers. After that late spring, there's still a lot of wheat in the fields. So did you solve the murder overnight?"

Orly rocked back on the back two legs of his chair and said, "Basically, I spent all night thinking about a sock, but that's not all. I was standing around next to Chuck Schultz and, give him credit, he kept his hands in his pockets and let the experts get on with their work, but he had been wandering around looking at the old dining hall. He said it reminded him of that case a few years ago. 'A genuine locked room mystery,' he called it."

Palmer, with his feet up on his desk, sadly shook his head and said, "Yes, well, Chuck. Not our most brilliant deputy. When God was ladling brains into his cranium, somebody must have bumped his elbow. I hope you are not basing your crime solving deductions on the observations of Chuck Schultz."

"Well, I admit that he is not the sharpest knife in the drawer. But still, those window doors to the balconies were all locked from the inside—every one of them. I checked. There is no way that anyone could open those doors from the outside. The locks are such that there is not even a doorknob on the outside. Nobody could have gotten in that way. Besides, if anyone tried to do that, he would need a very long ladder. That might look just a tad suspicious, don't you think? I suppose one could do some kind of *Mission Impossible* stunt and lower himself from the roof on a cleverly constructed harness, but I doubt it. The only other door opened to the room with the buffet. Obviously, since we couldn't get in until Swen Walstrom brought the key, that door was locked from the inside as well. From the evidence, no one could have committed the murder. And clearly, that is not the case."

"Orly, Orly, Orly. It's not the 1930s anymore, and people do not set up locked room mysteries these days just to baffle the detective. Remember me telling you about John Dickson Carr? He would write these mysteries that always included an impossible murder. And in almost every case, the solution was extremely simple, such as that Gherkin murder we had a few years ago. As I recall, that was the first murder case we ever worked together. Now, I can't tell you who done it in this case, but I can tell you how. Somebody waited until Kivi locked the door, or maybe the murderer locked it himself, then murdered the artist, then went out a balcony door, pulling it closed behind him, then somehow was able to lower himself to the ground.

"Yah, but …"

"Those locks are from the 1960s when air conditioning was added to the dining room. They have a small pull bar on the doors to close them. Back in those days, an enormous percentage of the people liked to have a cigar or a cigarette after a banquet. They would go out on the balcony to light up, or perhaps just to break wind. Because the air conditioning was on, they would use the small bar to pull the door closed after them. These locks had a little lever that they could move to unlock the door so that they could open it again. After any banquet, making sure those doors were locked, which involved moving that lever back in place, was something that was always done. But I talked to Harriet, and she said that she could not think of a time when anyone had shifted that little lever so that they could enjoy a breath of fresh air and get back into the room. I checked. I could move that little lever, but it was apparent that it hadn't been done for a long time. Consequently, I deduced that the murderer merely left by the balcony, pulling the door shut after him, and in doing so, relocked the door."

"But then, that would mean that …"

"Exactly. One of the guests at the opening, or even a member of the staff of the Arts Council, is the murderer. But which one? I don't think it will be that hard to find out."

Orly's forehead creased as he shifted his weight and the chair thudded on the floor. "And why would that be so"?

"All right, there are two ways to enter the gallery, since we have already dismissed the balcony entrance as extremely unlikely. There is a security camera trained at the front door, but unfortunately not on the door to the entrance of the dining room. Nevertheless, we have visual evidence of everyone who came into the gallery directly from the outside. The other entrance to the gallery is from the hotel lobby. It is necessary that this door be open because the restrooms are on the other side of the lobby. There is no security camera trained on this door, but there is a camera trained on the entrance to the lobby. Other than the two doors that lead to the ladies and gents rooms, there is a door leading off from the lobby that is used by the residents of the apartments on the upper floors to access the stairway and the elevator. This camera will show everybody who came in and left the lobby and the time that they did so. The viewing area of this camera also shows the door that provides access to the apartments. If one of the residents came down, decided to take in the reception, and then went back to his or her apartment, the camera will show that. Finally, there is one door that leads to the custodian's area in the basement and to the garage and another door that is perpetually locked that leads to a rear exit. The garage, including the garage door, is also covered with a surveillance camera. Nobody could come into the garage without being seen. There is a door on the south side of the basement that leads to a small patio, which has a table and a few chairs where the residents sit peacefully by the river in the good old summertime, but this door is in the surveillance area of the garage security camera. On the street level, there are two businesses that are part of the hotel building. The N.F. Field Abstract Company and H&R Block have their own entrances and no access to the hotel lobby. There is one other door between the lobby entrance and the gallery entrance. Swen Walstrom has assured me that this door is never used, and as far as he knows, he has the only key. In any event, it only leads to another access to the lobby, which would be observable. Finally, there is that exit door near the garage entrance that has a steep stairway to the main floor.

"Walstrom said that he began working here one year after the hotel was converted to apartments. At that time, new locks were put on the lobby door, and ever since then the residents have been issued only two keys—one for the front lobby door, and one for their individual apartments. He knows of only two keys to the door by the garage entrance, one in his possession and one in the possession of Helen Monroe. His key was on his chain the entire evening, and Ms. Monroe assured me that her key had been with her other keys in her purse. To be sure, her purse was in her office, so the killer could have removed it. But there was no way that he, or she, could have replaced it.

"Therefore, logically, all we have to do is note who came in, who left before the time of the murder—which we should be able to narrow down to a period of about fifteen minutes—who was there when the body was discovered, and who was not there when the body was discovered. There has to be someone missing. On the other hand, if the murderer played cool and re-entered the gallery, after not being filmed leaving it, that will be evident as well. Find this person and you find the murderer."

"But in that case," reasoned Peterson, "the killer must have taken the murder weapon with him, and left with it. There was no trace of anything that was found that could be connected to the crime."

"Well, he took most of it away with him, anyway."

"What do you mean, 'most of it'?"

"I promised to tell you about the sock. Well, you found the first clue almost right away. Remember when you mentioned finding sand on the floor?"

"Yeah, so what?"

"Our murderer kept a sock, loaded with a few ounces of sand in his pocket—or in her purse, for that matter. One can force the sand into the toe of a sock, give it a couple of twists, hold the other end of the sock, and swing hard. That blow killed Kivi, and after he was dead, the killer decided to make a nasty little tableau with the paintbrushes. I suppose there could possibly be some of the killer's DNA on the sock, but since the forensic team could find no fingerprints, other than those of Kivi, on the brushes, I suspect he wore rubber gloves."

"Did you have a chance to examine the sock?"

"Yes, I did. It could have come from my sock drawer. It looked like the kind of sweat sock that I buy from Target. Since Target sells millions of them, I do not think that we should waste our time trying to discover who bought a white sock."

"But you know," Orly said, "that might be something else that we can look for in the security videos. If someone has a large bulge in their pocket, it could actually be a sock full of sand."

"Possibly, but this is clearly a premeditated murder. It was a summer evening, and while some of the men did wear a light sport jacket, many of them did not. Nevertheless, a sock with half a cup of sand in it takes up a relatively small space. If the sand is spread out within the sock, before it is collected in the toe, it really does not take all that much space. Furthermore, one could always carry it in his shorts or tape it to his leg. The "sandy sock," furthermore, could easily fit in a woman's purse, either for her own act of murder or to serve as an accomplice. Still, that's a good suggestion. Keep your eyes open for it."

"Me?"

"Yes, of course. You're the one who grew up watching television; you're the one of the video games generation. The BCA should be arriving soon, to do a more complete examination of the scene of the crime and the area below the balconies. They will also collect the security images. We should be getting the videos any minute now. That should give you a great chance to find us a killer."

"What should we do in the meantime?"

"I have to do a press conference in about an hour—I heard we have at least five newspapers interested in this story. One of the television stations in the Cities sent up a camera crew, and, of course, our friends from Fargo/Moorhead are already here. Somebody has to do that, of course. Furthermore, I need some time to think about it. 'Little grey cells,' you know."

"So it's not just because you hate watching grainy videos, then?"

"Of course not. But while I'm sure we will have to do follow-up witness interviews, I see no reason to start going out and grilling people when we might be able to find video evidence that would point to the murderer. To be sure, that's only circumstantial evidence, but after we identify him, or her, I would expect we can bring that person in for questioning; we turn the screws and present him with the visual evidence, and we get a confession. There should be no need for prying into innocent people's lives. Meanwhile, let's take a little walk. I want to go back to the old hotel and check out that balcony to see if I can figure how in the heck anybody could get from a balcony that is fifteen feet high without killing himself."

It was a crisp and beautiful day, as so often happens after a prairie thunderstorm, so instead of walking directly to Mill Street, Palmer and Orly walked down Court Street and on down to the river. The River Walk is a three-block-long promenade by the riverside, featuring a walking path paved with decorative bricks. To be sure, Fergus Falls is not a noisy city, but thirty feet below the surface of the streets, the river walk suddenly becomes a place of solitude, with the only sound that of the rushing Otter Tail River and the tweeting of song birds.

"This is lovely," Orly said. "Do you come down here often?"

"Yah, almost every chance I get, in the summertime, at least. Sometimes Ellie will pack a lunch, and we'll meet up and sit on one of those benches and have a little picnic. Sometimes she even brings a bottle of wine, although we have to drink that a little surreptitiously. On a morning like this, it is a hidden jewel of Fergus Falls. Although I wish more people would enjoy it, I sometimes think I would like for it to stay hidden."

The two men walked up the steep lawn when they got to Mill Street and ambled over to the River Inn. They noticed with approval the yellow tape that had been stretched across the entry to the gallery and entered lobby. Helen Monroe and her staff had been ordered not to enter the premises and the two men walked in silence through the murder scene, noting once again the bloodstained floor. They opened the door to one of the balconies and stared down at the concrete surface. "You're still young and disgustingly fit, Orly. Think you could jump down from here?"

"I could if I had an overwhelming desire to break my leg. I suppose I could climb over the railing, grip the rails at their lowest point, and lower myself down, but it would still be a heck of a drop. An experienced paratrooper might be able to do it without ending up in the hospital, but I wouldn't chance it unless the building was on fire and I was trapped. I suppose that if I parked a convertible down there I could leap into it."

"Sorta like Zorro leaping from a balcony onto his trusted horse?"

"Yeah, something like that," admitted the deputy. "Let's take a look at it from below."

A few minutes later they stood looking up at the balcony and Palmer said, "It looks even more impossible from down here. Nevertheless, to quote our old friend …"

"I know, to quote Sherlock Holmes, 'When you have eliminated the impossible, whatever remains, *however improbable*, must be the truth.' In this case, leaving by the door that was locked from the inside was impossible, ergo, the murderer most certainly left by the balcony. Is that what you were going to say?"

"Er, well, I guess that was exactly what I was going to say. So, maybe … perhaps … well … check into that dumpster, see if there is an old mattress or bean bag chair or anything like that."

"Hey, that could be it," Orly said, and walked over to the dumpster. "It's empty!"

"Oh. Let's see, today is … I'll bet it has already been picked up. You're going to have to go down to the dump and see if you can find the 'sanitation engineer' who is responsible for emptying this dumpster."

"Me?"

"Of course. I've got the press conference coming up, and you don't have anything to do until we get the security videos. Let me know what you find." Orly grumbled most of the way back to the courthouse.

The press conference had gone as well as could be expected. By this time the sheriff was an old hand at obfuscation, and he did it with charm and grace. He extolled the Lake Region Arts Council, the Fergus Falls Police Department, the professionalism of the forensic team, and the impact of arts in Minnesota, and he hinted that progress was being made. He reported on the activities of the Bureau of Criminal Apprehension, and, in answer to a question of who would be leading the investigation, replied that under ordinary circumstances, this would be under the jurisdiction of the Fergus Falls Police Department. However, the chief was on vacation in Canada, and, in light of staff pressures, and in light of his previous experiences in homicide, he would be directing the investigation. In the end the reporters left with little more than the knowledge that Alek Kivi was dead and that the investigation was continuing. Everybody was satisfied.

Back in his office, Knutson occupied himself with paperwork, e-mail, and the *New York Times* crossword puzzle. At a little past his lunch time, he still hadn't heard from Orly, so he walked over to his office, looked in, and said, "Hey, Orly, how's it going?"

Orly sighed, "First of all, I found the driver of the truck that picked up what was in that dumpster. He said he didn't take a very good look at what was in there, but he did say it was practically empty. Since he had just unloaded it at the landfill, he could show me the exact spot where he had dumped it. Smelly place! Sometimes I realize that there are worse jobs than being your deputy. In any event, it was plain that there was absolutely nothing in that load that could have been used to break the fall of someone jumping from one of those balconies. Oh, well, good thought, anyway."

"Wanna go to lunch?"

Orly spread his hands across his desk and said, "As you can see, The B.C.A. just brought in the videos a few minutes ago, and I've just started looking at them. This is going to be a helluva job. The video is quite clear, fortunately, but people are moving around all the time. I checked the garage surveillance camera first. During the whole period of the reception, only four cars came into the garage, and I was able to locate on the lobby camera all of the people who were in those cars going up to their apartments. But the other videos! Uffda! That's going to take a lot longer. In any event, I think I am making some progress, and I want to work on this a little longer. Could you have Chuck Schultz go over to The Spot and get me a panini?"

In other circumstances, Palmer would have told him to get his own sandwich, but as he peered over Orly's shoulder and viewed the monitor of people walking in and out of the picture, the thought occurred to him, *Better you than me*. "No, I'll go myself," he said. "In fact, I might even get me one. Er ... bye then."

Returning with the paninis, Palmer discovered that Orly was in no mood for conversation, and so completely involved in his work that he did not even turn around when he grunted a "Thank you." *Could have offered to pay for his own lunch*, Palmer thought, but he left to find something else to do.

At five, Palmer checked in again. "Found us a murderer yet?" he asked hopefully.

This time Orly leaned back in his chair and took his eyes away from the screen. "Well, I think I am making progress, at least. It took me only a few minutes to discover that there would be no immediate answer to our question of who could have re-entered after the time of the murder. I started to study faces, faces, and more faces. Finally, I figured that if this were ever to be the primary mode of identifying a killer, then it needed to be done right and completely right if it were to be used in evidence. I started isolating each face in the security videos, and then making a copy of that face in a separate folder for purposes of identification. Naturally, I was able to identify many of the faces by sight, and a couple hours ago, I asked Harriet Monroe to come over and identify others. So far, I have only four people remaining to be identified. Of course, I took the names and addresses and telephone numbers of everyone as they left the building last night after the murder. To be sure, there were a few who left well before the murder that I was unable to identify, but obviously, if Kivi was still painting when they left, they did not murder him."

"I think we can safely deduce that," Palmer nodded.

"So far, however, I have yet to find anyone who entered and re-entered without leaving, which is what he—yeah, yeah, I know, 'or she,'—would have had to do. There were a few people whom I recorded as entering, leaving, and entering again. More than likely, they slipped out to smoke a cigarette or call somebody on their cell phone, but not during the time of the murder. So that shouldn't matter. Right?"

Palmer considered the question and cautiously replied, "I suppose that's true. Are you going home soon?"

"Of course not! I can't leave it like this! I just think the answer is right in front of me if I can only see it. Get me a cup of coffee if there's any left, will ya?"

So it's come to this, Palmer thought, as he poured some very elderly coffee in Orly's mug. I have become the serving boy to my deputy. *Nevertheless, as I said before, better him than me.*

CHAPTER TWELVE

"Love is the triumph of imagination over intelligence."

– H. L. Mencken

Sheriff Knutson took his time getting to the office the next morning, expecting his deputy to have prepared a report that would point out the inevitable conclusion that, based on the security camera evidence, a certain individual had committed the murder. He was therefore puzzled that Orly was not in his office. In reply to his inquiry, Palmer learned from his secretary that Peterson had not yet arrived at his office. Finally, a bit after ten a.m., Orly, without knocking, walked into Knutson's office and plopped himself down on a chair.

"So what did you discover, and what have you been doing this morning?" Palmer asked.

"As to what I have been doing, I have been trying to get some sleep. I was here until about three this morning. As to what I discovered, I discovered that nobody could have committed this murder. I have accounted for every single person who was there during that time. My final count was forty-seven people. I had the names of forty-three people who gave their information before leaving. You and I and Mrs. Kivi and her sister make forty-seven. None of this group left the gallery after the door to the 'artist working' area was closed. The security cameras did not show anybody re-entering without leaving. If we are to apply your treasured Holmes maxim, we would have to conclude that since it was impossible for any of these people to have committed the murder, the only remaining conclusion, no matter how improbable, leaves us to conclude that the murderer was a very large and dangerous mouse."

Palmer paused for several seconds while he stroked his chin and then said, "I do not tend to find the mouse theory particularly persuasive. Okay, well, it just means we haven't figured it out yet. We will have to solve this the old-fashioned way. I know that I didn't do it, and, sincerely trusting that you didn't do it, we have only forty- five suspects remaining. Where should we start?"

"As I recall, you have always made a point of getting to learn more about the victim. I got the impression, from what I heard in the hour before he was murdered, that Kivi was neither well respected nor well liked. Clearly, whoever bumped him off either hated him or feared him. Who benefits from his death? It certainly appears that he was not a wealthy man, and I presume that whatever estate he has will go to his widow and his children. We already have the means, if your idea of the sandy sock is correct, which I think it will prove to be, and we have the opportunity, sort of, but we just can't figure out what happened after the murder. I would think that once we find the motive, we will be able to draw some useful conclusions."

Palmer nodded, "Yah, I couldn't have put it better myself, so what kind of motives could cause somebody to not only murder a man, but to shove paint brushes up his nose?"

Orly shrugged and replied, "You'd think that getting home at three in the morning would mean I would fall right to sleep, but I didn't. I lay awake tossing and turning and seeing all those faces again. I tried to think which of those people would be compelled to violence. As I see it, we have quite a menu of motives. We talked about Kivi being somewhat of a ladies man, improbable as it may seem. A crime of passion? I suppose if he had dumped some besotted woman, she easily could have had a sand-loaded stocking in her purse. She could have had the strength to swing a cosh. Since we don't know how she would have pulled off the disappearing/reappearing act, we certainly can't dismiss this as something a woman could not do. On the other hand, if a man discovered that his wife was having an affair with Kivi, that could also be a motive.

"Jealousy?" Orly continued, "Did you hear any of those snide remarks by the other artists who were in attendance? I got the impression that there was a great deal of resentment that he, rather than they, had a one-person art show. Monetary gain? There could very well be things that we don't know about. Just because he dressed like a street person doesn't mean he didn't have a fortune in bonds or the deed to a gold mine, or that he was an heir to a fortune. Power? It might be hard to imagine a weasel like that having much power over anybody, but blackmailers, for instance, can gain a lot of power over their victims. Revenge? We might have something here. It was apparent just listening to comments that I overheard, that he had, at the very least, stepped on a lot of toes. It would take a very large foot or some very sensitive toes for that to be a motive, but who knows?

People are sometimes murdered for the flimsiest of motives. Clearly, we need to get a better handle on the victim."

"So ..."

"So we first talk to the person who supposedly would know him best. We've gotta talk to his wife."

"Right," Palmer said. I'll see if we can meet with her sometime early this afternoon. That will give you some time to get some caffeine in your system."

The Kivi home was about five miles east of Fergus Falls, just off Highway 218. When the sheriff had called Carol Kivi, she had agreed to receive them at one-thirty. As Knutson and Peterson drove out of town, Orly said, "Well, then, did you hear any good Norwegian jokes while you were in Norway."

"Curiously enough," Palmer replied, managing to disguise his annoyance, "they do not seem to enjoy stories that tend to poke fun at their own stupidity. Nor did I hear any Norwegian jokes in Sweden. Their lives are probably not as dour as Bergman films, and they certainly have a high standard of living, but they just don't seem to enjoy themselves all that much."

"Fortunately, while you were gone, I did hear a swell Norwegian joke."

Palmer sighed, "All right, I know you are dying to tell it. Get it over with."

"Right. Well, you see, Ole and Knute are digging this ditch, see, and Ole looks up and sees Sven just watching them. Knute says, 'Say Ole, how come ve gotta vork so hard digging dis here ditch and Sven, dat lazy Swede, yust stands dere vatching us?' 'I don't know, Knute. Dat hardly seems fair to me. I tink I'll go ask him.' So Ole, he goes up to Sven and says, 'Look here, Sven, me and Knute have been digging in dat ditch all morning, and yew yust stand dere vatching us. Ve don't tink dat's fair.' And Sven, he says, 'Well, Ole, it's because I'm the foreman.' 'All right, den,' Ole asks, 'how come yer da foreman?' And Sven tells him, 'It's because I'm smarter than you, Ole.' And Ole says, 'I don't tink dat's trew.' 'Oh, it's true all right, Ole. Come over here.' And Sven leads him over to a big tree and holds his hand up in front of the trunk and says, 'Here, hit my hand.' Ole winds up to hit him a good one, and at the last second Sven drops his hand and Ole smashes his fist into the tree. He goes back to the ditch, grasping his sore hand, and Knute asks him, 'Vell, did yew find out?' 'Yah, I did.' Ole says, 'It's because ve are too dumb.' 'Oh, Ole, I don't tink dat's trew.' 'No, it's trew, all right,' and Ole puts his hand in front of his face like this and says, 'Okay, Sven, hit my hand.'"

For one of the rare times, Palmer laughed out loud. He continued snickering for a mile or so and said, "You know, I don't think I could have appreciated that joke before that incident with those 'holier than thou' cops and all those drivers who tattled on me. I must tell that story to Ellie."

They were still smiling as they drove up to the Kivi home. Suddenly realizing that they were going to interview a widow, they almost literally wiped the grins off their faces and knocked on the door. As they waited for the door to be opened, Palmer was surprised to look around at the beautiful lawn, the flowers, and a well-trimmed hedge. That hardly fit the persona of what he knew of Alek

Kivi. Carol Kivi invited them in, and Palmer was pleased to see that her sister was still staying with her. The widow said, "The kids are over at their friend's places. Everyone has been so kind. It's a beautiful day, so how about if we just sit out on the deck. We don't, or didn't, I suppose I must get used to saying, get much of a chance to use it this summer because the mosquitoes have been so bad. But it should be all right now. Would you care for coffee or iced tea? I have both." Orly opted for the iced tea while Palmer automatically said coffee. Mrs. Kivi's sister discretely went back indoors, and a short time later Carol returned with the drinks and a plate of brownies. "These are from our neighbors. As I said, everybody has been so kind."

Both men were only too happy to accept, and made the appropriate comments indicating their contentment. Finally, as though Carol could stand it no longer, she asked, "What have you found out? Do you have any idea who could have done this dreadful thing?"

"At this point," Palmer said guardedly, "there is very little I can tell you. We have everybody we can spare working on this, and the Fergus Falls police are also doing what they can. We hope to be able to tell you more before too long. Meanwhile, it would help us to learn more about your husband"—Palmer had learned not to use phrases such as *late husband* any more than necessary—"to discover if anyone could have a motive for killing him. We realize that this might be painful for you to think about, but it really is necessary."

"I understand," Carol said guardedly, "but I think I'd like to talk about Alek. In many ways, he was so misunderstood by so many people."

"How do you mean, Mrs. Kivi?"

She thought for a while and then said, "It's just that, in a way, he was two different people. With me, and with Fiona and John, he was a totally different person than what other people saw. Please do not misinterpret anything I say to be a negative comment, but I think he basically had a deep-rooted inferiority complex. As an elementary principal, I have encountered several children who have, for various reasons—poverty, divorce, physical or mental abuse—lost whatever self-confidence they ever had. Sometimes they become withdrawn, but at other times they tend to lash out against what they see as an unfair world. I think, in many ways, Alek was like that."

With an appropriate degree of empathy, Palmer asked, "In what way?"

"I think Alek had come to accept his, well, his own mediocrity, but only among the children and me. He had a resentment against anyone who ever slighted him or his art. And yet, deep down he knew that he did not have much talent. As far as I know, I am the only person to whom he confided this deeply introspective self-evaluation. He never let it get to him while at home, and as far as the children were concerned, he was just a happy daddy, happily painting silhouettes or doing caricatures from photographs."

"And yet?"

"After college, he tried teaching eighth graders something about art. As a teacher myself, I always say that eighth grade is the hardest position of all, and only very experienced teachers should ever be allowed to handle the little monsters. They are loud, sometimes smelly, they are full of raging hormones, voices are changing, periods are starting, and they usually find the need to question authority. Indeed, if there were some kind of law that would send all eighth graders to the island of Madagascar for twelve months, most teachers would support it. Well, Alek got a job as an eighth-grade teacher. Just out of college, beggars can't be choosers. A couple years of that, and he just had to get out. That was when we moved to that small town in Kansas where Alek got his master's degree. It took him a long time, and countless slights and insults, before he accepted that an M.A. from a little Kansas college was hardly the same as a Master of Fine Arts degree from someplace with a little prestige. When he finally accepted this truth, I think he felt, well, I suppose, it was 'a mediocre degree fit for a mediocre artist.'"

"But he must have had some artistic talent," Palmer protested. "As I walked through your living room, I saw several nice pieces on your walls. Is that still life with irises a Thill, by any chance?"

"Yes, it is. Are you familiar with her work?"

"You bet! Quite a few years ago now, she had a one-artist show at FFSU. My wife and I just fell in love with another still life, and we look back on it now and think that was one of the best investments we ever made."

Mrs. Kivi sighed and said, "To tell you the truth, most of the art around the house is that of other artists. I was the one who bought that small Thill. I think Alek felt a little threatened by that, but then he met the artist. She was one of the few fellow artists who seemed to take an interest in his work, and that painting became his most prized possession. I imagine she didn't like his work any more than anyone else did, but she made him feel as though she did. I think he might have been a little bit in love with her."

"But you indicate that as far as the other artists were concerned ..."

"Basically, they made it clear that they held him in contempt. It hurt him, I know it did, and yet ... I've thought about this for a long time. And after he was murdered, well, I've thought about it even more. It seems to me that all of our lives we are challenged to take one of two paths. First, we can follow our dreams. The second choice, as I see it, is to take the course of least resistance. I really do wonder if Alek ever had any dreams. We met in college, and I knew what I wanted to do. I wanted to be an elementary school teacher. I was focused on that and achieved my ambitions. Alek, well, it seems to me that he always took the course of least resistance. He did better in art than he did in anything else, so he decided to be an art teacher. Eighth grade didn't work for him, so he thought it would be easier to teach college kids. Now, he did not strive to get a degree of any worth, just the easiest degree he could get. His heart was never really in art, it was in getting by. He found that silhouettes could work for him, and he could do caricatures, and if that could work for him, well, that was enough. And yet ... again ... and yet, for he really was a rather complicated man in some ways, he resented those who strived and studied and tried and failed, only to rise again. It was like he somehow felt that their superior effort and superior talent demeaned him. I suppose his inner defense mechanism caused him to erect this façade of a misunderstood and under-appreciated artist. But at home? With me and the kids? He was an entirely different person."

Palmer thought for a while, took a sip of his cold coffee, and asked, "Did you ever notice a particular episode with any fellow artist that, um, er, let's say, degenerated into the area of lasting hostility?"

"No, perhaps it might have been better if there had been such a thing. Perhaps a real rival, or something. But for the most part, his fellow artists seemed content to simply ignore him with contempt."

"Did he react to this 'contempt,' as you put it, in a way that would have created a real enemy, one that may have been tempted to end his life?"

"Among the artists? No, I can't see it. Why would they murder him when then could stick a small knife in his back every time they saw him? One doesn't murder somebody just because he is annoying. I suppose they could just be jealous because Alek made more money than they did with their 'oh-so-precious' creations."

"Is that right?" Palmer asked, with just a bit too much amazement in his voice.

"Well, I suppose when one considers their teaching salary, they might take home more money, but you might be surprised at the amount Alek could clear with his creations. I mean, those silhouettes basically cost him the price of a board, some black paint, and some varnish. He bought large plain tablets for his caricatures, and, of course, no precious metals or gems went into his jewelry. The markup on greeting cards was spectacular. So yeah, he made good money. Now, he ran his own business, just as I did my own work at Wellstone Elementary, so I can't give you a rundown on each aspect, but we have a joint checking account, and you would be amazed at how much he added, especially since last March, into our account."

"I wouldn't pry into this unless it was necessary, but was there a special reason why the amount rose in March?"

"I never thought about it before, but I just presume it was seasonal. There are very few venues where he could sell his art during the winter. He spent all that time building up his inventory, and then activities really picked up as spring approached."

Orly, chewing another brownie, paused and said, "We have become aware of other confrontations during the last few months. Apparently, there was some trouble with a child swallowing a dangerous dose of lead solder from one of his jewelry creations. We knew nothing of this at the time, but apparently the child became seriously ill and the father made some rather serious threats. What can you tell us about that?"

"Yes, Alek felt very bad about that. It had never occurred to him that the solder could be dangerous, and that professional jewelers used a different method. But when the girl's dad came to our house to confront him, Alek, being Alek, could not bring himself to simply be humble and apologize. Of course not. He had to get all high and mighty and spout some nonsense about artist integrity that only made the situation worse. I was afraid the man was going to attack him, so I got in between them. Alek did finally mumble an apology, but last I heard, a lawsuit was going forward."

"Do you think this person could have felt the need for revenge?"

Mrs. Kivi threw up her hands and shook her head as though she were attempting to clear her thoughts. "I don't know. I think I got him calmed down enough before he left. Besides, if he was thinking of suing Alek for his eyeteeth, why would he want to kill him?"

"You might be right about that," Orly agreed, "but I understand there actually was a physical encounter at the recent Otter Tail County Fair. What can you tell us about that?"

Carol rolled her eyes and said, "Ah yes, everybody's a critic. From what Alek told me, this guy was somehow insulted that Alek's picture did not make the guy's daughter look cute enough. Alek said the man just came up to him and hit him in the face. Knowing Alek, the man probably came up to voice his displeasure and Alek made some kind of incendiary remark about the man having no taste in art. But still, if a man goes so far as to sucker punch another man, do you think he lays awake thinking how to murder him as well?"

Orly said, "On the face of it, I would have to say no. Unless, that is, if your husband tried to carry the issue far beyond that. He was in our office wanting to swear out a warrant for assault against the guy, but since he could provide neither a name nor a very good description of him, we were unable to take any action. If he had discovered this man's identity, and made threats, and if the man had something that needed to be hidden from authorities, it might be possible."

"But still," Carol said.

"I agree, but still!" Palmer contributed. "On the other hand, I overheard a snippet of conversation the night of the opening that I found curious. It seems there was an architect who was upset that your husband had used, without permission, an image of a farmhouse that was an international award winner. He made several allusions to copyright and patent infringements—I didn't fully understand what it was all about—but he was clearly determined to have it out with your husband. Do you know anything about that?"

"Yes, I am afraid I do. It is another perfect example of Alek doing everything he could to get up another person's nose. The architect is a fairly well known professor of architecture at North Dakota State University. The whole thing could have been handled with an apology and an earnest interest in the professor's work. Naturally, Alek was confrontational and dismissive. He finally realized that his copying of the professor's work could get him into real trouble, so he did his best to alter the artwork that he had already produced and made sure he made no more. I can't see why he would want to kill Alek over it. If his career was so important to him, why would he want to ruin it by a nasty murder?"

"Why indeed?" Palmer asked. "But it does present a rather disturbing pattern. I mean, murderers do not usually behave in a socially acceptable or an intellectually justifiable manner. In our sometimes-sad profession, we have found all sorts of reasons for homicide, the vast majority of them totally insufficient to account for such a terrible act. One can claim that no one would murder another person just because he is annoying, but this is not always true."

A silence settled over the room. Palmer looked at Orly and Orly looked at Palmer. Carol looked at the floor. Palmer cleared his throat and said, "There is one other thing I must ask you about, and I recognize that it may make you uncomfortable to talk about it. Believe me, however, we would not probe into this issue if it were not, well, potentially significant. Are you aware of your husband having any, you know, relationships with other women?"

Carol Kivi smiled somewhat wryly and said, "I knew that you would have to ask this question. The answer is, unbelievably, 'yes and no.' Alek was never what you could call a 'ladies man.' In fact, I doubt that he ever had a real girlfriend before we met, and I can guarantee you that he did not have any afterwards. I sometimes wonder if, as we grew older, Alek regretted that he had not had a more, shall we say 'varied,' love life. And of course, the image of a Bohemian artist would have to include a more liberal social attitude toward married life. So when some unsophisticated lady would come to his tent and would be absolutely overwhelmed by the majesty of his barn and silo, he would flirt outrageously with her. I didn't particularly like it, if and when he told me about it, but it sure helped sales. This was a fan base like no other. Here were people who were actually impressed with him. There were several occasions where he would meet some woman for coffee or for a glass of wine. It boosted his ego immensely. It was his own little tiresome game, and it did no real harm. He even managed to have his undivided attention rewarded by a commission of 'our farm' or a caricature that looked far more lovely than the subject. So, in answer to your question, yes, I was aware of all his silly little flirtations, but no, he did not have what anyone could call a relationship with another woman."

Palmer asked delicately, "How can you be so sure?"

Mrs. Kivi smiled and said, "First of all, I know that he loved me. Sometimes love doesn't always make sense to people on the outside of a relationship. I have hardly thought of anything else for the last two days. This was a powerful, even all-consuming love between two people. There could never have been anyone else for him any more than there could have been anyone else for me. The second reason I am sure is that if he had had a relationship with another woman, I would have killed him."

This statement hung in the air like a bad smell while Carol Kivi pleasantly grinned at the two lawmen. They could not think of anything to say to that, and proceeded to thank her for her cooperation and hospitality. A short time later, they were on their way back to town.

"That is some lady!" Orly said. "I think she provided an insight into the victim's character more valuable than any court psychiatrist ever could. Still, in spite of what she said, it makes one wonder, doesn't it?"

Palmer had no doubt about what his deputy meant. "Yah, it some ways it makes the whole thing even more mysterious."

"Exactly. Even after hearing her defend her husband and extol his good points, and her insightful analyses of his character, I gotta admit, I still don't get it. How could a classy lady like that be passionately in love with a lump like Alek Kivi?"

Palmer laconically replied, "Women!" to which Orly nodded with deep understanding. "But you know," Palmer eventually continued, "there is still something that just doesn't add up. How come everybody in the world, except his wife and presumably his kids, detests this man? A Doctor Jekyll to three people and a Mister Hyde to the rest of the world? I think that her love for her late husband was genuine, but did it make her blind to his real shortcomings? Is it a case of an unwillingness to speak ill of the dead? Is it part of her vanity to make her weasel husband look better than he was so she looks better as well?"

Orly was nodding the entire time. "That's what I was thinking. That is, 'the lady doth protest too much, methinks.'"

"That Shakespeare?"

"Yeah, *Hamlet*, I think."

"And yet, she treated his art and his pretention with an almost brutal analysis. I have this feeling that she told us something, perhaps not even realizing it herself, that could be very important in discovering who killed her husband."

"I think so, too. So what do we do next?"

"I think we need to get to the bottom of just how Kivi came to have an exhibit at a rather prestigious gallery, which he proceeded to fill with rubbish. The Lake Region Arts Council office was allowed to open up again this morning. I think we should have a chat with Harriet Monroe tomorrow."

CHAPTER THIRTEEN

"Art is the most intense mode of individualism that the world has known."

– Oscar Wilde

The murder scene had been cleaned, and there was no trace of blood on the floor of the office of the executive director of the Lake Region Regional Arts Council. Nevertheless, throughout the day Harriet Monroe kept looking at the spot and shuddering—not an elephant in the room, simply a bare spot on the floor filled in with horrible imagination. When the sheriff and his deputy entered the room for their ten o'clock appointment, she noticed they both surreptitiously glanced in that direction. She sat them down and offered them coffee. They both accepted.

"I'm sure you noticed," she told them, "but we have taken down Kivi's *Magic in Minimalism* show. His widow actually stopped in and asked us to keep it up as a memorial to her late husband. We were discrete enough not to say that now that we had a chance to get rid of the hideous stuff we could hardly wait to do so. Instead, we showered her with sympathy—I mean, we really are sorry for the poor lady—but simply said that, under the circumstances, to do anything else would be inappropriate. To help her out, we did put a notice in the *Journal* that the contents of the show would be kept at our offices and that interested persons could still purchase his work. Apparently on the assumption that now that the artist is no longer able to produce his unique creations, the value of that work, just like

Picasso's, will skyrocket, we've sold four silhouettes and nine caricatures already this morning."

"Are you putting us on?" asked Orly, aghast.

Harriet sighed and said, "I rather wish I were. But it's true. Anyhow, I suppose I should be glad that the money will go to the widow and not to the artist so that no more boards can be vandalized and no more black paint will be wasted. But, whatever," she said, with an ease that reflected the mutual respect the existed between them. "What can I tell you about *Magic in Minimalism*?"

Palmer looked at Orly, and Orly looked at Palmer, and the sheriff finally said, "Well, and I don't mean this to be any sort of criticism, but how did it happen that you ended up with a show of the works of Alek Kivi?"

Harriet sighed and said, "It is really a bit hard to explain, or understand, for that matter. We had been all set to have a showing of the woodcuts of Sonja Danielsen, a Danish artist who is on the faculty of Gustavus Adolphus College. At the last minute, the Danish government—Ms. Danielsen is from Denmark—invited her to present her work at a national symposium in Copenhagen. Well, it was the dream of her life, and one that she just could not refuse. We could hardly blame her when she asked to cancel her showing here. So, that left us with about five weeks to either have a show or none at all. We had a meeting of the nine-member board, and they decided that instead of cancelling altogether, we would do a show of the works of Alek Kivi."

Both men nodded, and Palmer uttered an indistinct "I see."

"Yes, well, we tried to find a suitable replacement, and I contacted area college art departments and those in Minnesota that would be able to put up a show at short notice. This was unsuccessful. To tell you the truth, I was in favor of just cancelling the event. But this was a board meeting, and I serve the decisions of the Lake Region Arts Council. At our meeting to discuss what we should do, someone made a suggestion that we do a show of, as he put it, 'an ordinary artist.' He referred to our previous artists as being 'hoity-toity.' So this idea was kicked around for a while, until he suggested that one of the most ordinary artists in the area was Alek Kivi. Naturally, I was appalled."

Palmer interrupted to ask, "And who made this suggestion?"

Ms. Monroe thought for a minute and said, "As far as I recall, it was the Otter Tail County member, Bert Flom."

Palmer said, "Is that the guy who went down and got Swen Walstrom to open the door? Flom, like from Flom Home Appliances?"

"One and the same."

"And how was this received?"

Harriet roller her eyes and said, "To my horror, it was received quite positively. In fact, several members got quite excited about the idea, and pretty soon the term used was not 'ordinary artist' but 'people's artist.' One of our members actually has one of Kivi's dreadful silhouettes hanging in his living room, and he got all excited. At this point, Flom, who had never contributed anything since he got on the board, seemed to be carried away by his sudden importance and became somewhat of a champion of the idea. The tasteful member from Douglas County, a woman I might add, although I suppose that is irrelevant, was appalled at the idea, and the Clay County member was totally against it, although his sarcastic comments probably did not help matters. I am not a voting member, I am an administrator, and before I knew such a course of action was actually a possibility, a vote was called for, and the motion to invite Kivi was approved six to three."

"So," Palmer asked carefully, "how did you deal with that?"

"Ironically, it is not really that bad of an idea. Perhaps we are too 'hoity-toity' and too academic, and perhaps we do tend to ignore the, erm, 'people's art' that is all around us. One can see some marvelous art painted on a barn door, or a mailbox, or even a store window. Some people have an innate appreciation for art, a stunning sense of perspective, and an imaginative use of color that is just serendipitous! Unfortunately, none of these terms could be applied to the works of Alek Kivi. Why is art important? Aristotle defined art as the realization in external form of a true idea. It idealizes nature and completes its deficiencies."

"Exactly!" Orly chimed in, "To Aristotle, 'the aim of art is to represent not the outward appearance of things, but their inward significance.' I would challenge anyone to find inward significance in the works of Alek Kivi."

Palmer straightened up in this chair, raised his eyebrows in amazement, and gave Orly an approving glance. "Not only that," Palmer said, "but Picasso said something about art being 'washing the dust of daily life off our souls.' Looking at Kivi's 'art' I felt dustier."

This time it was Orly's turn to look at his boss with amazement. Harriet smiled and said, "I can't tell if you guys are extremely well versed in art appreciation or have been studying a *Bartlett's*. In any event, allow me to throw in a bit of Michelangelo—'The true work of art is but a shadow of the divine perfection.' If this is true, Kivi's work is little more than an act of sacrilege. But let's not get into metaphysics here, let me quote Salvador Dali: 'Drawing is the honesty of the art. There is no possibility of cheating. It is either good or bad.' Kivi's art was bad. Let's be honest. It stunk."

The sheriff couldn't decide if that was ending the interview on a high note or a low note, but there was no doubt it was an honest note. They thanked Ms. Monroe and proceeded to walk back to the courthouse. Again they chose to take the River Walk, and again they were temporarily lulled into silence be their surroundings. Finally, Orly asked, "So now what?"

"I was just thinking, when we come up at the end of the River Walk, we will be no more than a block away from Flom Home Appliances. It wouldn't hurt to drop in on Bert Flom to see what he remembers about that meeting."

"Sure, why not. It's too nice a day to hurry back to the office," Orly said. After a few minutes they walked into the showroom of the appliance store. Palmer spotted Bert Flom on the telephone and killed some time admiring a stainless-steel refrigerator, the kind where one can get ice and water directly from the door. He pined for just such an "icebox."

When Flom hung up the phone and made a note, Orly and Palmer sauntered over and Palmer said, "Mr. Flom? I remember you from that unfortunate incident a couple of nights ago. We were just over talking to Harriet Monroe and she told us about the meeting in which it was decided to invite Alek Kivi to show his work. Got a second to talk to us?"

Flom seemed to wince a bit, but said, "Sure, come into my office and sit down. Need any coffee?"

Palmer, somewhat reluctantly, declined, sat down, and said, "From what Ms. Monroe said, it was you who suggested that the board invite Kivi. Is that right?"

Flom made an exaggerated sigh and replied, "Yeah, I guess it was me. I had no idea it would cause such a brouhaha. People talked as though we had invited a chimpanzee to show his work and I got a lot of guff for it. We were just sort of kicking ideas around and I said that perhaps, just for a change, we should have somebody with more of an amateur status, you know, let sort of an ordinary Joe show his work. Pretty soon this was somehow translated into finding a 'people's artist,' and other people got caught up in the idea. I did too, I guess. Anyway, we were trying to think of somebody local, and I thought of that Kivi guy. I don't think I'd ever met him, but I saw him doing caricatures over at that Phelps Mill thing that they do every year. Everybody else seemed to know who he was, and we took a vote and decided to ask him."

"Did you ask him?"

"Me? No, that was Harriet's job. But everybody seemed to hold me responsible. I never spoke to the guy until the night of the opening."

Palmer nodded and said, "Yah, well, that's pretty much what Harriet told us, too. We were just walking around and thought we would duck in and ask you how things came about. It looks like you were kind of busy, so we'll just be on our way."

"No problem. Sorry I couldn't be of more help. By the way, I saw you looking at that swell stainless-steel refrigerator. I've got a great sale coming up next week."

"Yah, I like the idea of getting ice cubes without breaking up ice trays. Unfortunately, our current fridge runs just fine. I'll mention it to my wife, however. Thanks for your time."

Walking back to the courthouse, Orly asked, "So what should we do this afternoon?"

"Hard to say, really," Palmer replied. "We certainly are not very far into our investigations. With all of that video evidence, I thought I would be into necessary but tedious paperwork or a little bit of loafing by this time. I think, as long as we are looking at the art side of things, we should go up to FFSU and talk to the members of the faculty. After all, Kivi worked with them for a few weeks. I mentioned to the chair of the department, Wallace Duncan, that we would like to talk to them, and he said I could just call and he would set it up. He implied that late afternoons worked best, so maybe we can go over there later today."

"Why not?" said Orly. "It will give us another chance to talk to that silly Sherwin Williams. Are we going to interview them as a group or are we going to interview them separately?"

"Oh, separately. If there is one thing artists like more than to talk about themselves, it is other artists."

CHAPTER FOURTEEN

"To be instructed in the arts softens the manners and makes men gentle."

– Ovid

Knutson and Peterson entered the reception area of the Fergus Falls State University art department and spotted Wallace Duncan leaning over the secretary's desk putting final approval on a new brochure promoting *The Art Major at FFSU*.

"Oh good, you're here," he said. "I'll be with you in a minute. Just go into this conference room and I'll round up the others. Judy here, who makes great coffee, just made a fresh pot. Help yourselves."

Palmer and Orly entered the room to be greeted by a wonderful aroma. They each filled a Styrofoam cup and looked around. "State budgets do not extend to doughnuts," Orly groused. One by one, the members of the art faculty moseyed in, nodded politely at the lawmen, filled their favorite art-themed mug, and took their place around the table. At last Duncan entered and said, "Good, I see everybody managed to make it. That doesn't happen too often here, Sheriff. Perhaps you would like to say a few words as to how this interview should be handled."

"Yah, thank you, Professor Duncan. Thank you all for sacrificing your valuable time to speak to us. We'll try not to keep you too long. As you know, since I think you were all there earlier this week, one of your former colleagues was murdered at the River Inn. We would like to know more about his character and about your professional opinion of him. As you remember, the gallery was quite full that evening. That means there are a lot of suspects, not that we are accusing any of you. ... Yet!" Palmer smiled. The faculty did not. "In order to be more efficient, I suggest that I interview three of you and that my deputy here should interview the rest. Now, I suppose we could use this interview room, or we can come to your individual offices. Any preferences?"

Duncan waited for a response and then said. "I think it would be easiest to just go to people's offices. I mean, it is the beginning of the academic year, and everybody always has a certain amount of paperwork to do. This way they can just stay and work until you get around to them. Is there anybody here who thinks they have to get out of here early?" A rather tentative wave of the hand came from Clay Morton. "Okay, Clay, Deputy Peterson will come to your office and I will meet in my office with the Sheriff. I have a chair's meeting coming up in about twenty minutes, and I really should be there. Sherwin? Bonnie? The sheriff will be able to interview you after he is done with me. Denise and Maryann can meet with Mr. Peterson after he has interviewed Clay. How does that sound?" Everybody nodded their acquiescence, and chairs squeaked as the faculty proceeded to their stations.

Palmer followed Duncan into a large, rather messy office with hundreds of books and several rather startling framed photographs. "Nice office," Palmer opined, "and an impressive library." Academic types sometimes made Palmer feel defensive, so he added, "I've quite a few history books in my library at home."

"Ah, any art history?"

"Yah, my son took an art history class in college. I have this huge book that I find myself reading every once in a while. My wife and I have become much more interested in art the last few years."

Duncan feigned interest and plopped a gigantic book in front of Palmer. "This it?"

"Exactly. That's the one."

"Good text. I've used it for years. Now then, what shall I say about Alek Kivi?"

"What was your opinion of him as an artist?"

Duncan made no pretense at being diplomatic. "He was awful."

"How was he as a teacher in those weeks he taught for you?"

"Awful."

"How would you rate his general character or his relationship with his colleagues?"

"Awful and awful."

Palmer could not help but smile, yet kept his professional mien and said. "I may be misinterpreting you, but I get the idea that you did not think highly of the man. How about if I just let you tell me about him and where he fit in the art world?"

Duncan thought for a while and then said, "From the way I have answered your first questions, you may think that would call for a rather short and simple answer, but, in fact, in some ways he was a complicated individual. He did have a master's degree in art, but it is hard to judge just what it was that he learned. On the basis of that degree, and because he did have some teaching experience, albeit at a junior high school, we offered him a temporary job. Let's face it; we didn't have much choice. Now, far be it for me to criticize another institution of higher learning, I mean, professors sometimes have their own agenda that is, shall we say, not universally accepted but may still be valid. That said, he seemed to have a very poor grasp of the fundamentals of art. I say this with sadness for two reasons. First, because Fundamentals of Art 101 was the course he was hired to teach, and second, because he took that course at good old FFSU and apparently got an A in it.

"As far as his deep-seated aesthetic values are concerned, I'm not sure he had any. Instead, he seemed to have this, I donno, this 'low cunning' about what other people wanted. This has, as I understand it, made him somewhat successful in the flea market and county fair circuit. And, what the hell, as long as he kept to that and didn't bother anybody, who cared? His problem was that he always somehow managed to rub people the wrong way. I don't quite know how to put it except to say that he pissed off every human being he ever met."

"But did he, er, anger people to the extent that they would resort to violence?" Palmer asked.

"I doubt it. I mean, among the other faculty, we might have found him to be a pain in the ass, but we all knew he was temporary. It is amazing how much the human psyche can stand when you know it is only temporary. Just a few more minutes and the root canal will be over. Just one more crack of the whip and my fifty-lash penalty will be over. Or, more to the point, just one more week and Kivi will be gone for good. Among the students, well, you always hear things like 'He makes me so mad I could kill him.' Though of course I've never heard of a student actually doing such a thing. As chair of the department, of course, I had to deal with all the complaints. In one sense, it was probably good that he was only teaching 101. There were no budding senior artists whose career he could ruin. But violence from some source on campus, well, I doubt it."

The sheriff changed tack and said, "Yet I understand some members of your faculty felt that they had been somehow cheated from a showing that they thought they deserved. Can you comment on that?"

"Well, I suppose that would have to be Sherwin Williams. He has actually turned into quite a good teacher, but he still dreams of finding a unique style and becoming known for his art. It probably will never happen. But yeah, he was rather put out. He finally accepted the fact that he had been out of town when they tried to reach him, and has finally realized that they could hardly hold the spot open for him on a 'just in case' basis. He'll get over it. Furthermore, we were all there that night, and it seems to me that we were all sort of together most of the time. I think I would have noticed if somebody had slipped away to murder Kivi. I would have stopped them if that had been the case—half-heartedly, perhaps, but murder is just so tasteless a solution. Besides, just because somebody pisses you off, that's hardly a motive for murder. Look, I really gotta go. So if there is nothing else?"

"No," Palmer said, rising from his chair, "and thank you. You have been most helpful. Can you point me in the direction of Sherwin Williams' office?"

Palmer peaked beyond the open door of Sherwin Williams' office to spy him playing Solitaire on his computer. He cleared his throat and Williams, with a guilty expression, quickly put his computer to sleep. "Ah, Sheriff," he said, "nice to see you again. Under more pleasant circumstances this time, I hope." Williams, who had once been a suspect in the Gherkin murder investigation several years earlier, hastily rose to take a book off a chair. "Need any more coffee?"

"Now that you mention it, I thought you would never ask. That is really good coffee."

"For now, yes, but after a few hours, or days, for that matter, it tends to lose its appeal. I'll be right back."

Williams returned with coffee for both of them, sat, and asked, "So how can I help you?"

Knutson took his time looking around the office at some decent prints, some books, some portfolios that had not been picked up by students of the spring semester, and at the pictures of three children on the desk. Avoiding the question, Palmer said, "Now, I suppose that big kid is little Vincent, but who are the other two?"

"You remember the no longer little Vincent? I'm impressed. The older of the two girls is Mary, and the younger one is Frida."

"Let me guess," Palmer said, "Mary after Mary Cassatt, and Frida after Frida Kahlo."

"Exactly! I'm impressed again!" Pointing to a larger picture on the bookshelf behind him, Williams asked, "And do you remember Mae?"

"Of course I do. Is she still working in the registrar's office?"

"In a way. She is now *the* registrar."

"Ah, good for her. Give her my greetings, will ya?"

With a pleased expression, Williams said, "You bet. Now, I suppose you want to know more about Alek Kivi. To tell you the truth, I never got to know him very well. After all, he replaced me after my skiing accident, so I wasn't around much unless I decided to drop in to my office. In any event, he was only here a few weeks. I probably know his wife better, since our kids go to the school where she is principal."

"Well, what did you think of him?"

"I hate to be unkind," said Williams, who clearly didn't. "One does not want to speak ill of the dead, after all, but I found him to be, um, unlikable. I can't think of a particular run-in with the guy, but if my students happened to spot me in my office, they would come to me and complain. I have become a much more concerned teacher over the last few years, and mistreatment of students is something I just can't stand."

"Did you ever confront him about that?"

"No, but I'm sure I would have if I had seen him regularly. It's a funny thing. Sometime shortly after that unpleasantness a few years ago, I took stock of myself and my career. I wanted to be a famous artist and I guess I still do, but Mae and I finally took our dream trip to Europe, and I got to wander through the galleries of Paris and Amsterdam. There's this line from *Spoon River Anthology*—ever seen that play?"

"I think Rolf Norson put in on here, oh, I don't know, maybe twenty-five years ago, but I don't remember much about it. How so?"

"One of the characters—you remember they are ghosts in the cemetery—was Petit the Poet, who laments offering up his silly iambics 'while Homer and Whitman roared in the pines.' I decided that if my paintings were but silly iambics, I could still be of use as a teacher. I worked hard at it, and the result is that plaque on the wall."

Palmer put his reading glasses to read the inscription on the plaque, recognizing Sherwin Williams as the 2010 winner of the *I. Kenneth Smemo Excellence in Teaching Award*. Palmer said, "Wow!"

"Yes. It is awarded annually to recognize the teacher of the year for the entire university. I value that more than any painting I have ever created. And this is what bothered me the most about Kivi. I mean, his art was just atrocious; but just because I have not yet been able to create memorable art—note the 'not yet'; I'm still working on it—I at least can teach my students to recognize great art when they see it. It was like he didn't even try. And when he had them do projects for Art 101, he seemed to go out of his way to ridicule them. The freshmen of that class are seniors now, and a lovely girl, who really does have talent, was just telling me last month how she just about gave up art forever because of him. Bottom line, he was the most useless teacher and artist I have ever seen."

"And yet," Palmer said cautiously, "I understand that you created quite a scene when you found out that he would have a one-person show at the River Inn gallery."

"Ah, I suppose that you have been talking to Harriet. Well, I can't deny that I acted boorishly, and I am rather ashamed of it. But dammit, I still work hard on my art. Just because it is not of the same caliber of a Thill still-life, it doesn't mean I'm not still trying. And to discover that had I just been in town, had Mae and I not decided to take the kids to Disney World, I probably could have had a one-person show myself. And then to think that this warper of young minds, this cruel parody of an artist, was selected instead, I mean, I suppose I just lost it. I now understand exactly how it came to pass, and I have apologized to Harriet."

Palmer suddenly switched the tone of the interview by asking, "Would you say that your feelings about Kivi could be classified as violent?"

A few years ago, Williams would have been totally flustered at such a question, but now he simply replied, "I suppose you are asking if I felt such outrage that I became convinced that it was necessary to murder Kivi. It seems that there is no doubt that he aroused somebody to that kind of passion, but nobody would kill somebody just because he considered them to be a bad teacher and a horrible artist."

Palmer nodded and stood up. He tossed his Styrofoam cup in the basket and uttered his thanks. He concluded with a "Nice family you got there, Sherwin, and say hello to Mae for me. Now then, can you point me to Bonnie Lassey's office?"

Miss Lassey welcomed Palmer into a room filled with color. On one wall was an exquisite still life, on another wall was a small self-portrait, and on the third wall hung a giant abstract consisting of orange, yellow, and various shades of red. Palmer found it somewhat disconcerting, but at the same time rather exciting. He had seen Miss Lassey at the Kivi opening and, indeed, it could be assumed that every man in the room had noticed her. She looked to be about twenty-five years old, she was tall, and she had fine brown-to-auburn hair, green eyes, and the kind of figure that teenage boys dreamed about. She welcomed Palmer with a genuine smile but did not offer coffee. *That's just as well*, Palmer thought.

"How my I help you, Mr. Knutson?" she asked.

Palmer tried not to be caught admiring her figure and said, "I'm not really sure you can. How well did you know Alek Kivi?"

"I never met him. I just started at FFSU last year, so I was not here when he was here. I saw him through the open door as the 'working artist,' although I never noticed much work, and that was the only time I ever laid eyes on him."

And those are some eyes! thought Palmer, but he said out loud, "I presume, however, that you knew of him by reputation. How did others feel about him?"

"Perhaps it is unfair of me to say, since it relies only on the judgment of others, but everyone seemed to have a gut reaction of utter contempt, rather like Democrats have for Dick Cheney."

"Would you say, er, hatred?"

Miss Lassey clicked a manicured fingernail against her teeth, and thought about it. "Actually, I think that might be too strong. In fact, I think saying he was held in contempt, is a much more accurate assessment."

"Did you ever detect an undercurrent of dislike that could lead to violence? This might seem to be a leading question, but as an outsider, who had never met the man, you might have been able to pick up on the kind of, well, contempt, as you put it, that would have been shocking or at least notable."

"No, nothing like that. I don't think people get murdered just because they are intensely disagreeable. "

"Well, I'll leave my card with you. If anything occurs to you, do not hesitate to call me. Thank you for your time. It has been a pleasure meeting you."

Palmer made his way back to the reception area, and found Orly waiting for him. "Are you finished," he asked.

"Yup, just now. Are we going back to the courthouse?"

"Yah, we'll compare notes and see if anything jumps out at us. Oh, Judy," Palmer said, smiling at the secretary, "that was fine coffee."

Back in Palmer's office, Orly said, "Well, I will type up these interviews, of course, but just from my notes, I can't say that I learned anything."

"Nah, me either. Whadda you got?"

"I talked to Clay Morten first. He had the darnedest coffee mug that I've ever seen. It is a head of some kind of troll—just repulsive. In any event, just to put him at his ease, we talked about that and his other creations for a while. It seems that he is scheduled to have a one-person show at the River Inn next summer. He had just returned from a study in Spain a day before the murder, and he claims that he had no problem with Kivi taking the spot on the calendar, since he wasn't nearly ready. He sees the scheduling of the Kivi showing as an unfortunate thing that just happens sometimes and that he doesn't blame Ms. Monroe for it at all.

"He remembers the time Kivi taught at FFSU with undisguised rancor, and he had nothing but bad things to say about him as a person. And, in his words, 'I won't even insult the profession by calling him an artist.' He claims that he did not go into the room to watch 'the so-called artist at work,' and that during the time that the door was closed he, and most, if not all, of his colleagues, were drinking punch. He didn't come right out and say it, but he implied, with a considerable amount of profanity, that the murder served Kivi right and the world was better off without him. I tried to gauge if his dislike of the victim would have led violence, but he said that if he started to kill everyone who was an asshole, it would be like Sisyphus rolling the rock up the mountain. At that point, he abruptly said he had to go, and went."

Palmer grinned and said, "So you're implying that Morton did not like Kivi?"

Orly smirked and said, "Yes, that was the impression I got. So then I went and talked to Denise Steel. Now that is a woman who is not afraid to voice her opinions, not just about Kivi, but legislators who try to cut spending for the arts, pro-life women, people who can't grasp the significance of large sculpture and its importance to public places, the administration of FFSU, strip mining, the oil industry, endangered species, and I think that is just the tip of the iceberg, which, of course, she would use as evidence of global warming."

"Hmmm," Palmer said, "it sounds like she and Ellie would get along just fine. So what did she say about Kivi?"

"In order to save time, and to edit out some of the more earthy insults of the man, she 'hated him,' she 'detested him,' and he 'nauseated' her. I finally had to jump in and ask her whether, in her opinion, any of these traits could lead one to contemplate actually murdering Kivi, she actually paused for a bit before she finally said, 'Nah, he wasn't worth it. Nobody kills somebody just because they are obnoxious.'"

"I think it is safe to say that there is a pattern emerging," said Palmer, with a wry grin. "So then what?"

"I finally got a chance to speak with Maryann Stamp. She is a very quiet person—I suppose one could say meek. Well, from my perspective, I would say that if her kind inherits the earth, more power to them." Orly glanced at his notes and said, "Instead of ranting against that poor sap Kivi, she used words like 'his service as a teacher in our department was not very successful.' Or, 'I don't think that teaching was what he was cut out for; he did not seem to have the inclination to deeply care about his students.' Concerning his art, she said that he never seemed to 'strive to get better, or to try something new.' In many ways, her quiet, thoughtful assessment was every bit as damning as Denise Steel's diatribe. When I tried to probe as to whether she had seen anything or heard anything that might indicate a willingness to use violence against Kivi, she said something like 'I have never been able to understand violence in any form, and I'm not sure that I have ever witnessed it outside of movies or television, which I very seldom watch for that very reason. I think, for that reason, that I would be able to pick up on that far better than someone who lives, at least vicariously, a more violent life. I can't see anyone murdering Alek Kivi just because he was a, well, let's face it, a jerk.'"

Palmer proceeded to tell Orly about his interviews. "I'll write up my interviews, and all the interviews will be in the file, and perhaps we can return to them to see if there is some kind of information that might help us, but I doubt it. I think we both agree that we did not detect any kind of murderous intent among the lot of them. Besides, it seems that they all stuck together in a kind of solidarity display during the opening. If one of them had sneaked out to commit murder, I expect that it would have been noticed. But geez, I don't know what else to do but keep snooping around."

"So what's on tomorrow?" Orly asked.

"There are a couple of loose ends that need to be tied up. During the summer there were a couple of incidents, as you reported to me, that indicated that Kivi had made a few more enemies. Over the noon hour I got in touch with Scott Askelund. I got his cell phone number and called him. It seems they are spending the rest of the week at their cabin on Lake Lida. It appears that he was harboring violent thoughts at the time of the accident with his little girl, but he claims to have calmed down. In any event, I thought I should at least go and interview him. I thought I'd do that tomorrow."

"Just you? What should I be doing in the meantime?" Orly asked.

"Yes, well, just when is Allysha due?"

"A couple of weeks yet, how come?"

"And she can still travel in reasonable comfort?"

"I guess so. At least she hasn't complained."

"Good. I want you to take your lovely wife out to lunch in Fargo. I want you to take your own car, for which you will be paid mileage. The county will pay for your meal, but not Allysha's. Now, while you are in Fargo, I would like you to visit Professor Emil Holte at the North Dakota State Department of Architecture for a little chat. This guy claims that Kivi used images of his award-winning farmhouse for all of his silhouettes. He was at the opening, and he was quite willing to tell everyone that Kivi was a plagiarist and worse. I seem to remember him as being somewhat of a gasbag, and since he was prating about copyrights and things like that, I rather think that he was in the gallery for the whole time. Nevertheless, if anyone would know how to exit and re-enter an historic building, it would be him. So go see him, have a nice meal, and enjoy yourself. Go shopping for crib sheets or whatever else you might need. You can stay and take in a movie, for all I care. We'll talk when you get back. Now, it's been a busy day. Let's go home."

CHAPTER FIFTEEN

"I'm from Minnesota. I'm optimistic. I mean, that's just who I am."

– Thomas Friedman

Palmer usually made his own lunch, or just brought along an apple or a banana. This morning, however, as he walked into the kitchen to see what he could find, Ellie surprised him by handing him a paper bag and said, "Happy Anniversary, dear."

Palmer had a moment of panic. "But wait. Our anniversary is in May."

Ellie beamed and said, "Our wedding anniversary, yes. But this is the anniversary of the day I met a very handsome upper-classman for the very first time."

Palmer blushed and stammered, "Oh, oh, I'm so sorry, I had no idea of that date. How come you haven't mentioned this before?"

"I was going through a box of my old stuff, and I ran across a sort of diary of my freshman year in college. I started reading and, just about right at the beginning, when freshmen came for orientation, there was a mention of a boy named Palmer."

"You sure it wasn't Palmer Smith."

"I've only known one Palmer in my life, and one is enough. Anyway, I just thought I would make something special for you. Do not open it until lunchtime." Palmer, who hardly ever left the house without giving Ellie a kiss, made it a very long goodbye.

There was a small refrigerator in the break room, and to avoid temptation Palmer put away his lunch and tried not to think about it until noon. A reasonable few minutes short of that time, Palmer opened the bag and found a croissant with Black Forest deli ham, covered with generous slices of Emmentaler cheese, a hint of Grey Poupon, and a generous dollop of mayonnaise. A small bag of Cheetos accompanied this delight. *Oh, bliss*, Palmer thought, and proceeded to stain his fingers orange.

Palmer left Fergus Falls in the early afternoon and headed up highway 59, passing through Elizabeth and Erhard until he reached Pelican Rapids. He realized that the directions he had received from Scott Askelund were sketchy in the extreme, but he knew that he should take Highway 108 east out of town. Askelund said he was only about ten minutes out of Pelican Rapids. About forty-five minutes later, Palmer pulled into Askelund's driveway. He introduced himself to a barefooted young man who appeared to be wearing a bathing suit. "Care for a dip?" He asked. "I got a spare swimsuit."

Although it did sound rather good to Palmer, he declined, to which Askelund said, "Well, then, how 'bout a beer?"

Palmer grinned and replied, "I wouldn't say no!"

"It's too nice a day to sit inside," Askelund said. "Let's just sit under the ramada. That way I can look down and watch my wife and my little girl down on the beach. They don't really need watching, I suppose, since it is only a couple of feet deep there, but I enjoy seeing them have fun. Lida is a terrific lake. We love being on the east side. It is shady and calm in the morning, and in the evening we can watch the sun set or the thunderstorms roll in. In fact, we plan on gradually building on to this cabin and make it a year-round residence. One day, Colleen and I would like to retire here. I mean, this is Minnesota in all its glory. To be sure, this hasn't been the best of summers; I don't think it has ever even reached ninety degrees, but it still is glorious isn't it?" As he was reciting this particular psalm of praise, Askelund fished a couple bottles of Grain Belt out of the cooler.

As they sat side by side in canvas lounge chairs, Palmer enthusiastically agreed that it was indeed glorious. "Do you have a lake place?" Askelund asked.

"Nope," Palmer said. "We thought about it. But my brother has a place, and whenever we feel the need to do the lake thing, we can always go there. I was never much of a fisherman, but I used to do some water skiing in my younger days."

Askelund nodded and said, "We've been thinking about getting a bigger boat ourselves. We only have that little fishing boat now, but when Leah gets a little older, that kind of thing could be a lot of fun. But anyhoo, I suppose you are here to talk about that Kivi guy."

"Yah, I heard you had a little trouble with him. I understand you made a few threatening comments, something to do with him poisoning your daughter, I believe. Wanna tell me about it?"

Askelund batted at a mosquito and said, "Okay, well, I remember it was Memorial Day weekend. I took Leah with me to kill some time at that flea market south of Detroit Lakes. We stopped by this artist's tent and he was doing caricatures of people, and Leah begged to have her picture done. I talked her out of that, but then she saw this ring that she decided was Rapunzel's ring. I gave in and bought it for her. It was cheap enough and it seemed to delight her. So anyway, the next day she the ring came apart in her mouth—I don't know why she had her finger in her mouth—and she swallowed the stone. By that night she was sick as a dog and we had to drive to Fargo and take her into the emergency room at Sanford Hospital. The doctor told us that she had been poisoned by the solder the guy used to make the ring. I mean, the kid could have died, and she was in terrible pain that night. Clearly it was all the fault of the guy who made the damn thing. Make a cheap glitzy ring to appeal to little kids and make it out of toxic material! That's just criminal!"

Askelund took a long swig of beer and continued, "Well, naturally, I was pissed off to the extreme. I suppose I said some outrageous things about how the guy ought to be killed, maybe I even said I was going to kill him. People do say things like that in the heat of the moment without ever meaning them. I cooled down after a few days, but I still wanted to confront him. I went to his place and just wanted to rub it in how sick he had made my little girl and to give him a chance to, you know, beg forgiveness or something. Instead, he used the opportunity to tell me how stupid my little girl was to put his ring in her mouth and to explain that I did not appreciate fine art. I am not a violent man, but I almost became one then and there. Instead, I told him that he would pay for what he did. What I meant, of course, was that I would consult an attorney. I did talk to a lawyer that very afternoon, and he assured me that it was a very winnable action. The case was just about to be presented when I heard on the news that Kivi had been murdered. I suppose we could continue legal action in attempt to get money from his widow, but, I figure, she didn't have anything to do with it, so I'm just gonna let the whole thing drop."

"And your wife agrees?

"Sure. Besides, she never really had anything to do with the man. We went to the flea market again about a month ago, and Colleen went into his tent, without bothering to introduce herself, and noticed that all those rings like that were no longer being sold. Maybe little Leah's ordeal kept other kids from getting sick. I hope so anyway. Do you need to speak to either of them?"

Palmer took a long swig and replied, "No, I don't think so. Besides, it looks like they are having a good time, and the summer is coming to an end. Let 'em enjoy it while they can. Tell me, when is the last time you were in Fergus Falls?"

"Oh, it must be years now. We just never have a reason to go there. If we ever need anything, we can just go into Pelican Rapids or Detroit Lakes." There followed a long pause and a couple of mouthfuls of beer before he said, "Ah hell, that isn't exactly true. I had to go down for a meeting in Minneapolis last week, and I came home the night that Kivi was killed. I drove through town because the gas is a little cheaper there, and I wanted a quick sandwich at Burger King. I didn't know anything about Kivi's art opening, but when I read the story in the paper the next day, I realized that I must have been only a couple of blocks away when it happened. I wasn't going to mention it, but I've seen enough cop shows to know that gas stations sometimes have security cameras, and if you looked hard enough you could find some kind of receipt record with the time and everything. I just didn't want to waste your time and mine. I guess you could say I didn't want to sound suspicious. But other than that, it's all true. I hadn't been in Fergus Falls for years. In fact, I took the wrong street when I wanted to get out of town."

"I'm glad you told me, because, yah, we are in the process of checking every possible lead. More than likely, we would have found this out. I pretty much accept everything you said, however, so unless something else turns up, I don't think I will be bothering you anymore. Thanks for the suds, and go jump in the lake and play with your daughter. "

"Thanks, Sheriff, and good luck."

Palmer drove back to Fergus Falls and, since it was only about three-thirty, conscience dictated that he put in a little more work. He was shuffling papers when Peterson walked in. "Orly," he said, "I thought you were going to make a day of it in Fargo."

"So did I. But I met with that Professor Holte at eleven o'clock, while Allysha walked around Broadway a bit. I thought I would be going to the campus, but the architectural offices are right downtown in some kind of campus extension. Fargo has really changed—galleries, restaurants, and not an empty store front in sight. After the interview, I found Allysha again, and we went out to lunch. Very nice. Then we went to that big shopping center and looked at baby stuff. But after walking around for a while, Allysha said that her ankles were starting to swell, so we just came right home. I noticed your car in the lot and thought I'd just duck in to report."

Palmer nodded his head and said, "There might still be some elderly coffee in the pot, so get us a couple of cups and sit down and report then."

Orly returned a minute later with some vile black stuff in a cup, sat down, and said, "That Emil Holte is quite a character. I didn't realize how important he was in the field of architecture until, one, I saw all of the plaques and awards on his walls, and two, he had a chance to tell me. You were right when you classified him as a gasbag. An important, wealthy, and famous gasbag, but a gasbag all the same. Still, he was a nice enough guy. He showed me photos of his model farmhouse in several books, and pulled out various award certificates. There is no doubt that Kivi copied it directly to his silly silhouettes."

Palmer took a sip, grimaced, and asked, "Did he explain why he felt it necessary to drive all the way down to Fergus Falls just to be at Kivi's opening?"

"Sort of. He said that he wanted to make sure that Kivi was no longer selling pictures of his house on boards, which he claimed was an 'egregious example' of plagiarism and a copyright violation. He seemed to take delight in pointing out that Kivi had simply sawed off the offending house and remade the picture on a shorter board. He found that amusing and, if you can believe him, 'strangely endearing.' Personally, I think he was just as eager to go there and talk to anybody who would listen about how wonderfully his career had turned out. Clearly that is his favorite subject."

"So you don't see him as a murderer then?"

"Nah. He claimed he only made an issue of the whole thing to get Kivi to cease and desist. He had made noises to him about a lawsuit, but he said he had never even consulted a lawyer. I suppose if his gigantic ego and reputation were ever threatened, he might be capable of violence. But hardly over a matter like this. But as I said, in a way, I enjoyed our talk. And he told me a swell joke."

"All right, I can see that you can't wait to tell me. I probably couldn't stop you if I tried. Lay it on me. "

"Okay, things had gotten really crowded in front of the Pearly Gates, see, and there was getting to be a terrific backlog. St. Peter consulted God for advice. And so God tells him, 'Look, we got to get more of these people through. For today only, just ask everybody how they spent their last day on earth. If they had a really bad day, just let 'em in.'"

"'Well, if you say so,' St. Peter says, and he goes to the gates. The first guy comes up and St. Peter asks him to describe his last day on earth.

"'My last day on earth was my worst day on earth,' the guy says. 'I always made a point of doing rigorous exercises before I got dressed in the morning. I lived on the twenty-eighth floor of an apartment building. I would simply do my exercises in the nude because nobody could ever see me. So here I am, doing exercises, and I slipped and fell over the balcony.'"

"'Oh, that's terrible,' says Peter."

"'No, that was all right,' the guy says. 'I managed to grab on to the railing of the balcony just below me. I thought I was saved. When all of a sudden a man comes out and starts beating on my hands. I lost my grip and fell toward certain death.'"

"'Goodness sakes,' Peter says. 'What an awful day!'"

"'Actually, it wasn't that bad at that point' he says. 'I landed in some bushes, and they broke my fall. I was fine, with only my dignity damaged.'"

"'Well then ...'"

"'I looked up at the balcony where the man had smashed my hands, only to see him tip a refrigerator over the edge and it came down and ended my life.'"

"St. Peter said, 'That was indeed a horrible day, but heaven is, after all, Paradise. Enter, my son.'"

"So the next guy came up, and Peter asked him about his day. The man seemed a little bit embarrassed, but told him his story. 'I had long suspected my wife of having an affair. This morning, I decided to leave my apartment at the regular time, but I did not go to work. I waited until I saw the man, whom I suspected to be my wife's lover, enter our apartment. I gave them a few minutes, and then I banged on the door. My wife let me in and I dashed around the apartment looking for the lover, since I had seen him enter. I could find no one. Then, I looked out on the balcony and saw a nude man hanging on the rail. I ran over and pounded on his hands until he lost his grip and fell. I watched with satisfaction as plummeted to the earth. But then he landed in some bushes and was saved. This so outraged me that I ran into the kitchen and pushed the refrigerator over to the balcony and tipped it over. It fell directly on him. Unfortunately for me, however, this exertion was too much for me, and I had a sudden heart attack and died on the spot.'"

St. Peter was in a quandary. This man had taken a life. Still, it was a crime of passion, and there was no doubt that he had had a very bad day. Filled with misgivings, he opened the Pearly gates to him.

"The next man—I'll call him 'Ole,' for your sake ..."

"Oh, thank you," Palmer muttered.

"So Ole comes up, and St. Peter asks him about his last day on earth, and Ole says, 'It's kind of hard to explain, but here I was, sitting in this refrigerator ...'"

Palmer laughed. He laughed out loud and he laughed long. "Wonderful! And credit where credit is due, you told it marvelously well. With that, I think it is time to go home."

"Fine with me, but first, was there anything to be learned from that guy whose daughter Kivi allegedly poisoned?"

"Nah, I think that's a dead end. Nevertheless, it turns out that he was in town at the time of the murder."

"Really? That could be interesting. So what's on for tomorrow," Orly asked.

"As far as I know," Palmer said, "we have just about reached the end of anybody who had any kind of a known motive. You were the one who heard Wild Bill Bjerke make threats against his wife and 'her lover.' I think it's time we turn the screws on Wild Bill."

CHAPTER SIXTEEN

"Pray you now, forget and forgive."

– Shakespeare, *King Lear*, act 4, scene 7

The next morning Sheriff Knutson called Will Bill Bjerke and established a time for an interview. Bjerke was not enthusiastic about it, but he agreed that both he and his wife would be home at two o'clock. After a nice lunch at home with Ellie, Palmer picked up Orly in his Acura and drove to Bjerke's home. Orly was shocked at what he saw and what he didn't see. He didn't see a rabid dog threatening to attack him, and he didn't see the rusty pickup or two of the junked cars. As he approached the porch, he was pleasantly surprised to see that it had been repaired and painted. A ladder leaned against the side of the house where scraping, in apparent anticipation of a new coat of paint, was evident. They were greeted by a smiling Mrs. Bjerke, who, as Palmer had hoped, offered them coffee and "blond brownies."

It was a far more pleasant atmosphere than when Orly had been there a few weeks earlier. He noticed the deep red leather couch and the matching recliner upon which a healthy-looking Bill sat. A lovely new rug in a Navaho pattern graced the floor. When Orly complimented Betty on the new furnishings, she adroitly fielded his kind words and gave all the credit to Bill. The excellence of the weather was agreed upon, and Palmer finally said, "So, Bill, it seems that have turned your life around a bit since Orly was here last."

Bill returned a proud smile. "You bet. I've given up drinking, except for a bottle of beer now and then if I'm in the boat fishing with the guys. And you know what? Betty didn't even ask me to. I figured that I had been neglecting the finest thing in my life, and then when I started to think about how I belted her one, well, I felt so damn bad I had to do something. I never would have acted that way if I hadn't been drunk as a skunk. And you know something? I've never felt better in my life."

"Good for you," Orly said. "And I see you are even getting a little culture. I saw you at the opening of Kivi's exhibition."

"Yah, vell," began Bjerke, in his anxiety slipping into his natural Norwegian brogue, I yust wanted tew show Betty dat I vas totally over da whole ting, yew know." Strangely reverting back to American English, he continued, "I finally listened to her when she told me just what a fine guy that Kivi was. If I could show her that I was so confident in our relationship that we could go together and she could introduce me as her husband, then that would show her that she never again had to fear that I would haul off and slug her, you see."

"Did you have a nice time, or at least until the murder happed?" Orly asked.

"Yah, I didn't think I would, but I did. Betty took me back to where that guy was painting and introduced me to him. I told him how much I liked the portrait that he made of Betty, and we chatted for a while. He said that next time we went to the flea market he would do my picture. Of course, once I saw him I realized that she would never really fall for a guy who looked like that."

Betty remained mute and showed no reaction to this, but Palmer turned to her and said, "I'd like to know more about that time you shared a glass of wine with Kivi, not to suggest any kind of a mutual attraction, you understand, but to learn more about him. If you had a nice long chat with him, you might be able to give us some insight into his character."

Betty blushed slightly, but said, "All right. Bill and I have talked this all out, and I don't mind going through it all again. Alek and I talked the whole time he was doing my portrait. After he was done, there was no one else waiting, and so we talked some more. He just seemed so interested in me. He asked me about what I liked to do, and what I read, and my favorite things, you know, in a way that no one, including Bill, had done in years. I suppose I was just so flattered that somebody actually wanted to listen to me. I told him that it was a thrill for me to meet a real artist, and he said that he got his inspiration from 'the people,' people like me. I kept thinking about him for days, and when he called up and said he would like to talk some more, I discovered that I wanted very badly to do so.

"I thought Mabel Murphy's was a grand place," she continued. "It was just off the interstate, so it was handy, and it was a little nicer than other places. It was a real treat for me. As I told Bill, the thought of a romantic meeting did occur to me, and I found the thought exciting. As we sat there, I was kind of waiting for him to, you know, make his move. But he didn't. There was never anything like that. Instead, he told me that he really didn't have many friends, and that he had enjoyed talking to me and felt that he had made a friend. He proceeded to tell me all about his wife, who sounds like a real gem, and he bragged about his children. This time, I guess, he did most of the talking, like he just wanted to talk about, or even justify, his art. To tell you the truth, I got rather tired of it, and, not to speak ill of the dead, but I could see why he didn't have much in the way of friends. But he bought me wine, and it was delicious, and I really did like him. At the end, he said something rather curious. He said something like 'I hope you didn't think I asked you to share a glass of wine in order to start some kind of an affair. I'll leave that kind of thing to my sister-in-law and her big-shot businessman.' Of course, I have no idea who his sister-in-law is, or who the big-shot businessman is, and the last thing I wanted was to get into that."

Palmer looked at one of them and then the other, and asked, "Were you at the gallery the whole time from when you entered until we let everyone leave after giving their name and address?"

They both affirmed that they were, but after a few seconds Bill said, "Yah, but I sneaked out for a smoke a couple of times. I mean, just because I gave up drinking, nobody said I had to give up smoking."

"And when was that?" Orly asked.

"I guess the first time was not too long after we got there. I was going to grab a quick one before we went in, but Betty doesn't care for it much, so I thought I'd wait until she found somebody to talk to and then sneak out. The second time was just after they closed the door and said that Kivi was going to spend a little time getting ready for his talk. I was gone a little longer the second time. I walked over to the bridge and looked down on the water. I like doing that."

Palmer and Orly met eyes in recognition of the potential importance of that statement, and Palmer asked, "While you were out there, did you happen to see anyone else who might have been in the gallery coming back, like maybe he had also ducked out for a smoke or something?"

"Now that you mention it, I did. I don't know who he was, I'd never met the man, and I don't remember seeing him again. How so?"

Palmer waved in the air and said, "It probably isn't important. We're just trying to get a handle on where everyone was at the time of the murder. Orly, do you have any more questions?"

"No, but I must just say that these brownies are delicious, Mrs. Bjerke."

"I'm so glad you like them," she replied. "Let me wrap up a few of them to take back to your office."

Orly made a half-hearted 'tut-tutting' sound and let Betty go into the kitchen. The men all stood up and made their way to the door. Wild Bill said his goodbyes and started walking back to the house. As Palmer and Orly got into the car, Betty came out with a plastic bag full of brownies. She went to Orly's window and said, "I just wanted to say how very grateful I am to you for what you did for me that night. You have saved our marriage and—who knows?—maybe even my life. What you did and what you said could not have been more perfect." She smiled at Palmer and said, "and maybe one day, when this old guy here decides to retire, I can vote for you for sheriff."

During the short trip back into town, Palmer and Orly discussed the case. "Do you think Wild Bill could have done it?" Palmer asked.

"Sure. If you had seen him that night, you would not put anything past him. To be sure, he was pretty tanked up, but a predisposition to violence does not, in my experience, ever quite go away. If he is turning his life around, good for him. If he is not, well, who knows what demons still lurk under the surface."

"Absolutely. It would be nice to trust him, but he did have a motive, no matter how much he may say he completely believes his wife. And he was on the spot. The problem with this case is that we have so many people with minor motives. Fellow artists, a guy whose daughter was poisoned by accident, an offended architect, a wife who may or may not be satisfied with her husband's little peccadilloes, or a husband who may or not believe that he is a cuckold. But the one thing that keeps coming back to me is what we have heard in so many different forms. 'Nobody murders someone just because he is a pain in the patoot.'"

CHAPTER SEVENTEEN

"Mid pleasures and palaces, though we may roam,
Be it ever so humble there's no place like home."

– John Howard Payne

It had been two weeks since the murder. As far as the media were concerned, it was a "dead" issue. There were no longer reporters hanging around the courthouse, and it was no longer mentioned on the television news or the newspapers. And why would it be? There had been no progress. Orly had succeeded in discovering the identity of everyone at the opening, and he had interviewed every one of them. The file was thick, but the information was thin. The people of the Lake Region had other things to do.

School had started, and Mrs. Kivi was keeping busy with the activities of the new academic year. At Fergus Falls State University, classes for the Fall Semester had started, and it looked like a promising season for the Flying Falcons football team, and coach Francis Olson was preparing his team for the first game. Old Rolf Norson was planning another exceptional year of college drama, and the art department enrollment was at an all-time high. In the ditches by Maplewood State Park, the sumac was already turning a brilliant scarlet. Days were getting shorter and the geese were looking to the south. In the sheriff's office, Palmer Knutson did little active work on the Kivi murder case, but he still thought about it all the time. In the back of his mind, he was sure he had heard enough to figure it all out. There had to be something there. Why couldn't he put it all together?

The morning routine at the Knutson home had changed over the past year. The absolute delight of the day had been to get the daily *Minneapolis Star Tribune,* read about the Vikings and the Twins, and doing the *New York Times* crossword puzzle. There was nothing that brought greater bliss than holding a fresh newspaper in his hands. But times change. He now owned an iPad and Ellie owned a Kindle. He discovered that he could get the *Strib* online for pennies a day. He could save over $300 just by reading it on his iPad. So every morning, he did not even have to open the front door to get the paper. He got up, went to the bathroom, made coffee for himself and Ellie, brought two cups back to the bedroom, and crawled back into bed. They sat there side by side, reading the "paper" without having to share the sections. For the most part, Palmer hated it. His hand got tired holding the annoying thing up, he frequently touched the screen in the wrong place and temporarily lost the article, and, while not unpleasant, perhaps, it just didn't feel right. After a while he would get up, hit the shower, go down to the computer, and print a copy of the crossword puzzle. Coffee, breakfast, and the puzzle was still a pretty civilized was to start the day.

On this morning, Palmer was still somewhat groggy. It had taken him a long time to drop off to sleep, as he mentally went through the interviews and all that they knew about the Kivi case. It was a Thursday, which meant that the puzzle was not particularly hard, but often tricky. He tried to concentrate, but his mind kept wandering. What did he know about the case that he couldn't see?

Ellie noticed that he had not filled in a square for some time and asked, "Difficult today, dear?"

"Huh? Oh, yah, they always have some tricks on Thursday. Words spelled backwards or upside down or something. I donno, I just can't see it."

"Are you ready to cheat and look up the answers?"

"No, but I think I'll put it away for a while. Give it a fresh look later on."

"Are you going to take it to the office with you?" Ellie asked.

"Yah, I might, but you know, I think I feel like going home for a while this morning. I need to organize my thoughts about this Kivi case." Ellie knew what that meant.

Palmer had grown up on a farm east of Fergus Falls, about four miles from Underwood. He needed to calm his brain, and so he slipped a CD of Debussy into the player. Whenever he heard *La Mer*, he imagined himself peacefully floating in a boat on a Minnesota lake. Palmer parked his Acura and walked over tall grass that had once been a lawn. It was a spectacular morning, sunny with a painting of light cirrus clouds in the sky. It was so very quiet. There was not even the sound of a tractor to be heard. In a week, the farmers would be combining beans or corn, but not today. On a nearby electric wire, a mourning dove perched, and its call was exactly as it had been so long ago. It had been a farm like every other at the time, with a house, a barn, a chicken coop, a hog house, and a two-holer outhouse. Now, there was nothing to identify it as a place where three generations of Knutsons had lived but a windmill and a hole in the ground. The windmill no longer pumped water, but the vanes still turned and sometimes emitted a forlorn squeak. The hole in the ground was the basement of his old house, now a repository for fieldstones for the agricultural entrepreneur who farmed the land. He looked into space, to see just where his bedroom window had once been. On summer nights, with the window open, he could hear the sound of the train going toward Fergus Falls. He would dream of the places it would take him. On winter nights, he would listen to the stories his grandfather told of Norway. He smiled as he thought of just what he would have thought of Norway today. On spring nights he thought of baseball, and on fall nights he dreamed of football. *Well*, he thought to himself, with a smile, *I guess that hasn't changed.*

    A scraggly rosebush was still producing blossoms, just as it had done for sixty years. He walked over to it and, carefully avoiding the thorns, plucked a flower. He put it to his nose and thought, *Today's roses just don't smell good anymore.* What a wonderful childhood he had spent here! Parents who loved him, an older brother who looked after him, aunts, uncles, and neighbors who cared! He mused sadly about the child abuse cases that came to sheriff's office with depressing regularity. He sat down on what had been his front steps, now leading to nowhere, and looked toward the line of box elders that had been planted as a windbreak so long ago. He remembered that time one summer when a storm had blown a large tree over. He seemed to remember that he was about eleven at the time, and had turned the inside of the fallen tree into his hideout. His father had bought the first family TV, a seventeen-inch Crosley "Super V." Palmer had been a real buckaroo in those days, watching Gene Autry, Roy Rogers, and Hopalong Cassidy every Saturday morning. Every fall he would look forward to when the

Sears Christmas catalog arrived. He would always turn first to the cap guns. Glorious cowboy guns! He spurned with distain the sissified Roy Rogers guns, with rhinestones on the holsters. He longed for a double set of six-shooters in plain black holsters, and one Christmas he got them. Oh bliss. He recalled playing cowboys and outlaws with his school friends. They would point a gun at each other, shoot, and then stage a dramatic fall in the throes of death. "They got Smitty!"

    Guns had fascinated him then, and when he was in the army he was an MP and always had a pistol strapped to his side. He thought that was cool. Then. He continued to wear a side arm when he was a deputy and even occasionally after being elected sheriff. Now, he never did. He tried to remember the last time he had even been out to the firing range, and realized that it was when he brought a new deputy out just to show him where it was. In fact, it had been years since he had shot a gun. Over the years he had seen teenage kids using guns to hold up convenience stores, ordinarily sane motorists who resorted to guns in moments of road rage, and a three-year-old boy who found a gun in his father's bedside table and proceeded to shoot his mother. He realized that he now hated guns! But, dammit, those were swell cap guns! Enough! He decided to turn his attention to the Kivi case.

    At least he tried to. He found himself thinking about the Viking's preseason, little Bjorn, his grandson, whether or not Trygve would get back together with his girlfriend, what kind of something special should he get Ellie for Christmas this year, was it time to buy new tires, and gradually began to think of

Orly and Allysha. There should be a new Peterson on the planet any day now. Orly was a good man; he was glad that they had become friends as well as colleagues. He smiled as he thought of the age difference, and about how he really did enjoy ribbing him about being a Swede, and about how he had to continually accept Orly's Norwegian jokes. Gradually, he began to reflect on what measures they had taken to solve the Kivi murder. He remembered Orly thinking he could leap down off that balcony and land in a convertible, "just like Zorro leaping on his horse." His mind wandered. *... no ... not a convertible ... a truck ... what about a truck ... or a tall van ... somebody could just drop down onto the top of a truck ... like a delivery truck ... get down and drive away ... so who would have a truck?*

Then he started to think about that odd art reception that had preceded the murder. He tried to cast his mind back to what he saw, or more importantly, what he had heard. "Who do you suppose he had to blackmail to get a show of his own?" ... If there was one thing that seemed to be universally agreed upon, it was that Kivi's art did not deserve that kind of recognition. "She may have been the very first resident." ... Who said that, anyway? He also remembered Walstrom saying that the locks were changed a year after the first resident moved in. But he didn't say that all the old keys had been collected. Well, why would they be? They wouldn't be useful for anything except, maybe ...

"One doesn't murder somebody just because he is annoying." ... "You would be amazed at how much he added, especially since last March, into our account." ... "I never spoke to the guy until the night of the opening." ... "He seemed to have this, I donno, this 'low cunning' about what other people wanted."

… "Nobody kills somebody just because they are obnoxious." … "He seemed to be carried away by his sudden importance and became somewhat of a champion of the idea." The fair? … An affair? … "I don't think people get murdered just because they are intensely disagreeable." … Affair, affair, "… sister-in-law and her big-shot businessman." … "Nobody would kill somebody just because he considered them to be a bad teacher and a horrible artist." … "Who do you suppose he had to blackmail to get a show of his own?"

Palmer nodded. As certain as the fact that Ellie would never vote for a Republican, as certain as the fact that the Gophers would not win the Rose Bowl, as certain as the fact that Orly would never wear a wrinkled shirt, and as certain as God made little green apples, he knew who the murderer was.

He got back into his Acura. Debussy would not cut it. He put in Handel's "Hail the Conquering Hero" from *Judas Maccabeus.*

Back in his office, he explained to Orly the entire case against his suspect.

"So, no doubts?" the deputy asked.

"None whatsoever. One final certainty came when I drove by his place on the way to my office. The truck was there. I had seen it before, and I almost commented on it, because it looked so nice and new. I saw it, but did not 'see it,' if you know what I mean."

"So then," Orly said, "Are we going over and arrest him?"

"No, because we can't. We do not have a single piece of evidence. Not a single physical clue. Not a single witness. We can know something to be true beyond all reasonable doubt, but if we can't prove it in a court of law, it is useless. The only thing we can do, and I'm reasonably sure that this will work, since he is not a hardened criminal, is to bring him in and force, or trick, or cajole, him into confessing of his own free will. It's time to pay Bert Flom a visit.

"We'll just take my car. No use to get him all concerned with having a sheriff's car pull up in his driveway," Palmer said. "He's probably home having a relaxing lunch, and I'm sure we will be having a relaxing chat. We had a rather peaceful conversation with him when we visited him at his store, and I would guess he is feeling quite satisfied that we do not suspect him of anything."

"Are you going to take you gun with you?" Orly asked.

"No reason for that. Besides, I see you have your trusty Glock with you, as usual. Don't you ever get tired of carrying that thing around with you?"

"Forewarned is forearmed, as they say," Orly replied. "By the way, you look rather spiffy."

"Yah, but I figured that if I put on a suit it would just lend a little, you know, gravitas to the situation."

CHAPTER EIGHTEEN

"It seems to me most strange that men should fear,

Seeing that death, a necessary end,

Will come when it will come."

– Shakespeare, *Julius Caesar*, act 2, scene 2

During the short drive to the Flom residence, Palmer began to ponder that "gravitas" feeling. They were going to charge a man with murder, a man who, as far as anyone knew, had never had a parking ticket or an overdue library book, a lifelong resident of Fergus falls, and a respected businessman. Could he really have no doubt of the man's guilt? Was he sure? The sheriff decided he was. But would Flom really confess of his own free will? In his mind, Palmer rehearsed several ways to approach the task ahead.

Breaking the tense silence, Orly asked, "Do you think he has any idea that we are on to him? I mean, when we show up at his door, do you think he will know it is all over for him?"

"Who knows? Sometimes, in the case of someone who is not a habitual criminal, you run into a situation where the person is so overwhelmed by his appalling actions that his conscience begins to take over and he is actually relieved to be arrested. He wants to be arrested just to get it all over with. Let's hope that is the case here."

They parked in front of the large, rather stately old Flom home. They rang the doorbell and a few seconds later Flom answered the door, chewing on a sandwich. "Ah, Sheriff Knutson. What can I do for you?" he asked.

With a neutral expression on his face, Palmer answered, "May we come in for a few minutes? We just want to clear up a couple of things concerning the Kivi matter."

"Of course, of course," he said as he ushered them into the living room. "Need any coffee?"

"No, no. Just had some," Palmer replied, sitting easily on a soft leather sofa. "Actually, it might be better if we could ask you to come with us to our office. You remember that there were a ton of people there that night. We have a security video part of the gallery at the time of the murder, and we haven't been able to identify just who the members of the board were. You could help us a lot."

"Sure, sure," Flom said. "I tell you what, though. My wife is in the basement, so I'll just pop down to tell her where I'm going. Be back in a sec."

Flom disappeared in the direction of what Palmer presumed was the basement steps. Palmer and Orly looked at each other and shrugged as if to say, "That was easy." After a few seconds, however, Palmer heard a noise from an upstairs room. It appeared Mrs. Flom was not in the basement after all. Something wasn't right. He began to feel uneasy.

Flom soon appeared wearing a light jacket, although it was hardly cool enough for it. He walked over to the sheriff and pulled out a .38 revolver and put it to Palmer's head. "No. We are not going to the office," Flom growled. "Don't you move a muscle, Deputy, and leave that gun in its holster, or your boss gets his brains blown out. Knutson, you and I are going to take a little ride."

"For God's sake, Flom," Palmer said in a shaky voice. "You don't want to do this."

Flom's eyes were wild as he snarled, "Yes I do. You have left me no choice. I'm not gonna sit in some cell for the rest of my life for killing a guy that needed to be killed."

"All right, all right. Take it easy. I am unarmed. I'll do whatever you say."

"That's better. And you, Deputy," Flom spat out as he briefly waved the gun at Peterson, "don't you even think of following us, or the sheriff gets it. Understand?"

Palmer had never been so scared in his life. To be sure, someone had once fired a shotgun in his general direction, but since he had never seen the gun, he had had no time to be frightened. His knees shook, sweat was forming on his brow, but he attempted to project an image of serene calm. He said, "Do what he says, Orly. And do not follow us. You heard him. He does not want to sit in a cell, so we won't even bring up the subject of a cell any more."

Orly kept a blank face, nodded, and said, "Whatever you say, Sheriff." Palmer was certain that Orly had gotten the message that Palmer had his cell phone in his pocket and that it would be turned on so that it would be possible to trace him at all times.

Flom kept the revolver at the back of Palmer's head as he forced him out of the house and into Palmer's car. "Get out of here and drive. I'll tell you where to go," Flom said, adopting the persona of a tough guy with nothing to lose. Holding the gun pointed at Palmer's belly, just low enough so that it could not be seen from the outside, he said, "Just ease it into drive, go nice and slow, and take it to the Interstate."

"Want to tell me where we are going?" Palmer finally asked.

"Since you're the driver, I suppose it doesn't hurt to tell you. We're going to Canada. Just go to Fargo, get on I-29, and we'll be at the border in three hours. No need to call attention to ourselves by speeding. Just keep a nice steady pace."

"Whatever you say," Palmer said, and calmly asked: "By the way, do you have your passport with you?"

"What do you mean, passport? I don't need a passport to get into Canada."

"You do now. It's all part of the new rules of the National Security Administration. When's the last time you've been in Canada?"

Flom, somewhat confused by the chatty tone of the sheriff, replied, "Oh, I donno, maybe ten years or so. Why?"

"Well, you used to be able to just show the Canadian border guards your driver's license and tell 'em you weren't bringing any guns over the border, and they would wave you through. It strikes me that you have a bad combination of having a gun and having no passport. It's not going to work, Bert."

Flom thought about this for a while, and when exit 50, for U.S. 59 came up, he ordered Palmer to take it. After a while, Flom asked, "So how did you figure it out? How did you know it was me?"

Palmer, breathing a little easier now, said, "To be honest, I knew for sure it was you when you put a gun to my head."

"Oh God, what have I done! So you had no idea?"

"Oh, I wouldn't say that. I pretty much had it all figured out this morning. But, you see, we had no evidence. Not a scrap. We couldn't arrest you just on a theory, even though it turns out it was a pretty good theory. I suppose we could have charged you, but if you had found yourself a good lawyer, well, I don't know that we could have gotten a conviction."

"Son of a bitch," Flom muttered. He remained silent for a long while before finally asking, "So where did I slip up?"

"I gotta admit it was pretty clever. First of all, the murder itself was a masterpiece of planning," Palmer said, and noticed a somewhat proud expression on the face of the killer. "What made you think of a handful of sand in a sock?"

"I don't know. I suppose I read about it somewhere. Pretty effective, though, wasn't it?"

"Well," Palmer replied, "it certainly turned out to be. But you know, with that weapon, you gotta hit the guy in the head just right. I don't suppose there was anybody to practice on, so you might have gotten lucky there. Where did you keep it during the opening?"

"I wear briefs."

"Huh?"

"You know, underwear that fits right up in your crotch and has a little pocket for your private parts. Let the shorts hang just a little low, and you can easily have room for a sock with a little sand."

"And how were you able to sneak up on Kivi?"

"That was easy. I just ducked behind the screen and sat at Harriet's desk for a while. I had my telephone in my hand, and if anyone had peeked in there—which I didn't think they would do, and they didn't—I would just have pretended that I had ducked in there to make a phone call. I mean, I'm on the board, after all. Of course, Kivi had his back to me, and people came in and out all the time. Nobody stayed for long. I mean, who would actually want to watch him paint? So anyway, when he made a big thing out of closing the door, I could just softly approach him from behind. The fool actually made things much easier for me by locking the door. I had planned to do that as soon as I conked him, and that part was a little risky, since anyone could have come in, but in any event, I didn't have to worry about it."

"And the paintbrushes? A little dramatic, wasn't it?"

"Maybe, but I wanted to make sure he was dead. I hated the rotten weasel, and I actually got a charge out of slamming those brushes up his nose."

"And you wore rubber gloves, I suppose. What did you do with them?"

"I stuck 'em into my shorts, just where the sand filled sock had been. I just put 'em in the trash when I got home," answered Flom, sounding increasingly pleased with himself.

"You know," Palmer continued, in a friendly and complimentary manner, "The whole business about how you got off the balcony had us puzzled for a long time. Nice truck, by the way. New Ford E-Series, isn't it?"

"It is a swell truck. I did a lot of research on trucks before I bought it. Some of the appliances are getting so big these days, that the old truck just wasn't big enough. That refrigerator that you were looking at the other day, for instance, I couldn't have gotten in our old van. I was kind of lucky there, too, in that I had just gotten the truck a week before the opening, and hadn't gotten around to have 'Flom Home Appliances' painted on it. I could just park that under the balcony and nobody would know it belonged to me."

"Yah," Palmer said, in what by now could have been a conversation about fishing, "that gave us some trouble. Not a single witness could recall a truck being parked there. Now granted, when those drivers come up to the garage door, they are looking at the garage door to see that it is opening as it should, and they have no reason to look around, and I suppose a small white truck with no writing on it can be pretty anonymous. But still, you'd think at least one of them would have noticed it. I noticed, by the way, when we were talking to you at your store, that you seem quite fit for a guy your age. I didn't think anything about it at the time, but I imagine you just climbed over the railing, dropped to the roof of the truck, got in and drove away."

"Thank you. Yeah, I try to work out about three times a week. That was the neat thing about that truck. I drove away in my car, so even my wife wouldn't suspect, parked it at the back of my store, drove the truck to the old hotel, let it sit there for a while, and then used it to get down from the balcony, just as you said. I merely had to take the truck back, jump in my car, park it near the gallery, and get back in."

"Well, that was another thing that really had us stumped," Palmer said. "By the way, mind if I turn on the radio? I like to listen to Minnesota Public Radio while I drive." Palmer hoped for some soothing music that might calm Flom down. *Music has charms to soothe the savage breast*, he reasoned, and he wanted the calmest possible finger on that trigger. He was in luck, the music was Debussy.

"There were only supposed to be two keys to that rear door, the one that opens to a stairway to the main floor. But then I remembered someone talking about how they had turned the hotel into apartments, and that his mother had been one of the first to stay there. Looking back on that conversation, I was pretty sure that was you. Anyway, Swen Walstrom told me that they had put new locks on the apartments and on the outside doors about a year afterwards. But not new locks on all the doors. I reasoned, that it was just possible that there might be an old key laying around, and that it would have had to come from someone with a connection to one of the earliest residents. So, you just parked the car and went to the back door, let yourself in, climbed the stairs, opened the door, peeked in and did not notice anyone watching you, ducked into the gents' room, and came out cool as could be."

"Yup, that's about the size of it," Flom said proudly.

By this time they had passed through Pelican Rapids and were continuing north. "You know," Palmer said, "since I didn't plan on being kidnapped today, I didn't fill my tank. I mean, I have enough gas to get to Detroit Lakes, but then we're going to have a problem. How are you going to do that? It's going to be hard to hold a gun on me and run the gas pump at the same time, isn't it? And besides, most of the stations now have a security camera, and if you use a credit card, or even force me to use mine, that's going to leave a trail of evidence, too. Think about that!

"You know," Palmer continued in a chatty manner, "one of the most difficult factors in solving this case was motive. It turns out that everybody disliked Kivi, maybe even hated him. But as one of the people we talked to said, 'Nobody kills somebody just because they are obnoxious.' In fact, we heard that in one form or another from just about everybody. I suppose in your case, it was the blackmail, wasn't it?"

Flom suddenly turned cagey. "Maybe. I'm not talking about that."

"Why ever not? That's probably your one mitigating circumstance. He was blackmailing you about your affair with his wife's sister, wasn't he?"

"How in the world did you find that out? We were so careful. It was extremely important that my wife did not find out!"

"Actually, we never really did find that out. It was just a guess on my part. But, I suppose I know it now."

"Do you think my wife has to know?"

"Bert, Bert, that is the least of your troubles. Anyhow, the way blackmailers usually work, they demand a onetime payment to keep their mouth shut, then ask for a little more, then it becomes a regular payment, and maybe they ask just a little something extra. In Kivi's case, I presume he found about that Danish woman cancelling her show at the gallery and decided to force you to get him an invitation. Was that the way it came down?"

"Yeah, that's just the way it was. He asked for three hundred dollars to keep his mouth shut."

"Three hundred bucks! That wasn't much!"

"No, but pretty soon he realized that himself. He demanded five hundred the next month and for the next two months. As much as anything, it made me realize what an ass I had been. I ended the affair, and so he promised that the money payment would stop in exchange for that last favor. I suppose he would have broken that promise eventually, too, but it was the last chance I had to get out from under him."

After a minute or two of silence, Palmer said, "You know Bert, maybe things aren't as bad as they seem right now. I mean, you'll have to go to prison, no doubt about that, but you've never been in trouble with the law before. You were being blackmailed by a real scoundrel, to be sure. How long you get will depend on the skill of your lawyer and the mood of the judge, but I'd be willing to bet you could be a candidate for early parole. And I'm very aware that you are holding a gun on me, but you don't really want to kill me, do you, Bert?"

"I will if I have to, have no doubt about that. I've already killed once, and since there is not capital punishment in Minnesota, how much worse can it be?"

"Killing a sheriff? Are you kidding? It could be much, much worse. Think about it, Bert. Every cop, every highway patrolman, every park ranger, every deputy, and everyone who loves law and order will be looking for you. Are you going to kill them all? How many bullets do you have in that thing, anyhow?"

"You only have to be concerned that I have enough for you," Bert snarled. Then he lapsed into silence. They had reached Dunvilla. Bert said, "I need a little time to think. I've got a lake home on Pelican Lake. I'll give you directions. Turn left here."

Pelican Lake is a large lake, one of the finest in Minnesota. The size and number of lake homes represents a significant source of tax income for Otter Tail County. While the Flom home did not match the majesty of some of the "cabins," it was still an impressive structure. Palmer pulled into the driveway and, without asking, turned off the car. "Nice place," he cheerily said.

Flom smiled and accepted the compliment. "Yes. We've had it for two generations. And now I'll lose it all. Get out of the car!" Flom's face suddenly turned more menacing as he waved his pistol and ordered, "Go down to the dock." They walked in silence. In spite of the danger, Palmer could not help noticing that it really was a splendid day, with bright sun and just a few fluffy clouds. A light breeze created small waves that made a pleasant and rhythmic sound as they splashed against the bottom of the dock. The thought occurred to him that it was just such thoughts that people who faced the firing squad, the noose, or the guillotine supposedly had. When they reached the dock, Flom commanded him to keep walking. Palmer began to contemplate that with such a close distance, he would never hear the shot before the bullet entered his head. He decided he preferred it this way. As he neared the end of the dock, Flom asked, "Can you swim?"

"Um, yah, a little, I suppose."

"Good. Now give me those keys." Palmer handed over his keys. The question of whether or not he could swim gave him some hope. Flom took the keys and said, "Thanks. Nice car, by the way. Now keep walking until you get to the end of the dock. Hold it right there. You're right, Palmer, I don't want to kill you. But you are going to jump in the lake and stay there."

"Can I take my shoes off first?"

"No! I've already said I wasn't going to shoot you. I want to leave you in the lake with wet shoes so you don't just swim out and start chasing after me. I can see you from the house. I'm going to duck in and get a couple of beers. I really need one. If you're still in the lake so I don't have to shoot you, I'll even leave one for you. No hard feelings, sheriff, but I hope never to see you again."

"Take good care of my car!" Palmer yelled after him.

Three miles south of Dunvilla, a motorist traveling on Highway 59 would have seen a curious, perhaps even alarming sight. Three vehicles from the Otter Tail County Sheriff's Department and two Minnesota Highway Patrol cars were stopped together at a small paved area at the side of the road. Eight peace officers were gathered in a circle discussing strategy. Minnesota Highway Patrol officer John Hanson asked Deputy Orly Knutson, "So how long should we stay here? I mean, this is your call and we will do whatever you think is best. I just need to tell other officers in the area what we plan to do."

"Curiously enough," Orly said, "Palmer and I actually discussed just such a situation a few months ago. We had both seen the same movie—I can't even tell you want it was now—in which a Los Angeles cop had been taken captive with a gun to his head and his sergeant had to figure out what to do. Of course, in the movie, the sergeant had done wonderfully well, and we agreed that in such a situation it was better not to take any chances and to let time be on your side. I might point that the movie cop was very smart, but then so is Palmer Knutson. Okay, we know that Palmer's cell phone is still working, and we know that it has stopped moving somewhere near Pelican Lake. I think we should just wait here until it starts moving again. What do you think?"

Everybody agreed that was the safest course, but a few minutes later Orly said, "Uh-oh, the phone is no longer giving off signals. Palmer could have just shut it off, fearing that if it rang he might be in danger. More than likely, however, Flom discovered it and shut it off, destroyed it, or threw it in the lake. Finally, knowing Palmer, he had neglected to charge it up for several days and the battery just went dead."

"So what do we do?" Officer Hanson asked.

"If Palmer still has a gun pointed at his head, the last thing we want to do is stage some kind of heroic strike on a suspected position. I think we should wait a bit. Perhaps the phone will come on again, perhaps it won't. But let's get everyone else in on this. See if you can get a patrol car to be at the junction of

Highway 10 and 59. Let's call the Detroit Lakes Police Department and have a car on east Highway 10 just in case he decides to go through town. If you can't get a highway patrol car on highway 34 west of Pelican Lake, call the Clay County Sheriff's Office or the Barnesville Police to cover that area. Remember, it's Palmer's personal car, totally unmarked. It's a black 2005 Acura TL, license plate number 076 LVX. We are not dealing with an experienced felon here, and that may make his actions puzzlingly unpredictable, but I'm pretty sure we can keep him confined in this area. We will do what we can do under the circumstances, and that is wait. If we don't get a signal in half an hour, we might have to go to the last reported location of the cell phone. Personally, I will put my faith in Palmer Knutson."

CHAPTER NINETEEN

"All men that are ruined, are ruined on the side of their natural propensities."

– Edmund Burke

Palmer proceeded to tread water until he saw his beloved Acura pull out of sight. He relaxed and was disgusted to discover that the water came up only to his armpits. He waded ashore, sat down on a log, emptied out his shoes, wrung out his socks, took off his coat and tie, and laid them in the sun to dry. He fished out his cell phone, but, as he feared, it may have been smart, but it was not waterproof. He was sure that Orly had been able to track him, however, and that, although they would proceed with extreme caution considering the sudden disappearance of the signal, they would be along shortly. He walked barefoot up to the cabin, forced the door, and searched for a telephone. He found one, only to discover that it was disconnected. "Everybody has cells these days," he muttered. He proceeded to find the beer that Flom had considerately left him, and returned to the sunshine to wait.

Forty minutes later, he heard a car in the driveway and looked back to see his Acura returning. Bert Flom said not a word but went into the house and came back with a couple more cans of beer. He sat down next to Palmer and said, "I filled up your tank in Detroit Lakes. I figured it was the least I could do."

Palmer nodded his thanks, and for the next five minutes they sat in total silence. Finally, Palmer said, "Do you have your cell phone with you? I really should call Orly."

Palmer calmly informed his deputy of his exact location, and said he was in no danger and that the situation was under control. He informed Flom, "He'll be here in ten minutes, as will several other officers from all over. You've led them on quite a merry chase."

"Ten minutes?" Flom gasped, but how could they get here that soon?"

"Yah, well, you see, I left my cell phone on, and they have been tracking us ever since we left Fergus Falls. When I jumped in the lake, the signal quit, so they stopped near Dunvilla to see if it resumed. They were probably only about a quarter of a mile away when you got back on Highway 59. Naturally, I saw no reason to tell you this. I mean, how was I to know at that point how you would react? But at least you might have the consolation of knowing that nothing you did or did not do would have had any effect in making your getaway."

"Another beer?"

"Why not?"

Cars from the Otter Tail County Sheriff's Department and from the Minnesota Highway Patrol soon filled the drive. In spite of Palmer's telephone assurance, most of the lawmen advanced with guns drawn, and were surprised to see the barefoot sheriff sitting on a log with a can of beer in his hand. Palmer and Flom stood up and Palmer said, "I suppose it is that time. Bert Flom, I arrest you for the murder of Alek Kivi. You have the right to remain silent. Anything you say or do can and will be held against you in a court of law. You have the right to an attorney. If you do not have an attorney, one will be appointed to you. Do you understand these rights as they have been said to you?"

Flom nodded, but Palmer said, "Please answer the question verbally."

"Yes."

The murderer was handcuffed and led away to a secure car. When the prisoner had been driven away, Orly came up to Palmer and resisted, with difficulty, the urge to give him a big hug. Instead, he just put a hand on his shoulder and said, "You had me very worried. That was a pretty scary time. I didn't want to frighten Ellie, but I thought I owed it to her to keep her informed, and I've been keeping in touch with her throughout the whole ordeal. I just called her now to tell her you were safe and would be coming home."

Palmer reached up and covered Orly's hand as it lay on his shoulder. "I knew I could count on you; I never had a moment's doubt that you would understand that reference to a 'cell.' You're the best, Orly. I've been in this business for a long time. I've really only been shot at once in my life, and that resulted in getting one shotgun pellet in my hinder. But there is nothing like having a .38 shoved against the back of your head to engender real fear. I thought I was going to have to change my shorts, although I probably should leave out that observation when I speak to the media. Let's get back to town so I can put on some dry clothes."

As Palmer walked back to his car, Orly said, "Where do you think you're going? I'm going to have Chuck Schultz drive your car back to Fergus Falls. You're coming with me."

The thought of Chuck Schultz driving his Acura was no more reassuring to Palmer than having a murderer on the run driving it, but he eventually agreed. Orly, knowing Palmer's taste, had tuned the radio to Minnesota Public. A lovely, peaceful composition by Eric Satie was playing. Eventually, Palmer said, "I thought I had pretty much relaxed after a refreshing swim and drying off in the sun, but you know, this isn't something one can get over in a hurry. I was planning on going home, changing clothes, and going back to the courthouse to release a statement. What the heck, you know as much about the case as I do. You can release a statement and schedule a news conference for me at, let's say, about eleven o'clock tomorrow. What I would like now is to put on a pair of jeans, a T-shirt, my slippers, and sit outside with a humungous gin and tonic."

Orly smiled. "You talk as though you have some choice in the matter. When I bring you home, do you think for one minute that Ellie—or me for that matter—would let you go back to work? Other than joining you in that gin and tonic, if I am invited, that is, I don't expect to see you until tomorrow. After all, it hasn't been an easy day for me either. I was in danger of losing my boss and my best friend."

It was Indian summer, one of those warm days after the first frost. The hoopla surrounding the arrest of Bert Flom had long ago died away. It would be months, of course, until the trial, but that was not Palmer's concern. He had turned his attention to wasting Sunday afternoons watching the Vikings, doing his crossword puzzles, and pondering whether or not he should buy a new snow blower before winter set in. The office seemed to run itself, although Orly had taken parental leave to spend some time with Allysha and his baby girl named Elna. One day at noon, Ellie packed another fine picnic lunch and they found themselves on a bench along River Walk. The trees were just past their autumn glory, and leaves regularly fell down upon them. The river gurgled and muted whatever sound might be heard from the street. "Penny for your thoughts," Ellie said.

"I suppose I could take that offer," Palmer said, "but I wish it were the old British system where I could give you a ha'penny in change. I'm afraid my thoughts are not worth much. But I was thinking about other murder cases in which I have been involved. The key to so many of them was character—either the character of the murderer, or the victim, or both. I mean, I've come across victims of such low character that it was a wonder that somebody hadn't bumped them off years earlier. I've known a victim of such pure character that no one should ever have killed him. I've known a murderer who was a fine upstanding lady, and others who were genuine villains. In the Kivi case, the murderer was not a good man—after all, he committed murder—but he wasn't really a very bad man either. The victim, judging by his wife and family, had his redeeming points. We kept hearing things like 'Nobody kills someone just because they are annoying.' And I think that sidetracked me for a while. In the end, it seems he had some personal integrity and possessed a measure of honor as a family man, but he was also a two-bit conniving blackmailer.

"I grew up in a Scandinavian community that held a common attitude as to what one should do and what one should not do. One should not put himself pridefully forward, but should let his deeds and action reflect his basic honor. One should do what the community expects of him. I served in the military police force that emphasized honor and the difference between right and wrong. I became an officer of the law to enforce all of those values. Looking back on my life, I suppose I was somewhat of a prig in those years, expecting everyone to think and act as I thought they should. Over the last few years, however, I've generally come to believe that—how do they say it? 'People can do anything they like as long as they don't do it in the streets and frighten the horses.' Remember that old movie, *Anatomy of a Murder?* In it, Jimmy Stewart says something along the lines of 'People aren't just good and they aren't just bad—they are many things.' There are so many tiresome shibboleths that one hears during a lifetime. 'Time heals all wounds.' No, it doesn't, certainly not always, anyway. 'Time wounds all heels' and 'The wheels of justice grind slowly, but they grind exceedingly fine.' No, not always. I have known people who have done the worst possible things, totally without honor or personal integrity, even if they were not illegal, and proceeded to live the rest of their lives with no consequences. Still, if ninety-five percent of the people have a bad opinion of somebody, like Alek Kivi, I think they are generally right. There just seems to be something missing in their humanity, whether this is because of nature, nurture, or both. Maybe it is by accident or by choice or both. Who knows?"

A silence settled in between them, broken by the sound of falling leaves and running water. Palmer reached over and held Ellie's hand. "Perhaps it was by accident that we met that day, but it was by choice we loved each other. I can't say that it was God's hand that brought us together, but I can never deny that I have been blessed."

"We! We have been blessed."

Without a care of what the voting public might think of their sheriff had they been watching, Palmer and Ellie shared a gentle and soft kiss. "Soulmates!" he whispered.

"Soulmates," she replied.

THE END

Made in the USA
Charleston, SC
10 July 2015